NAKED
SHOULDERS

Virginia Bollinger
with
Cindy Regis

NEWMAN SPRINGS PUBLISHING
320 Broad Street
Red Bank, NJ 07701

First originally published by Newman Springs Publishing 2021

ISBN 978-1-63692-185-3 (Paperback)
ISBN 978-1-63692-186-0 (Digital)

Printed in the United States of America

This book is dedicated to Angela Wolfe and Julie Rucker.

Childhood

The grand buildings adorned with carvings of angels and gargoyles seemed to be swooping down on the little girl as she sat alone crying on the cold hard steps of a New Orleans gambling house. In the twilight, you could see her wet blue eyes. No one came to dry her tears or chase away the imaginary demons. The shadows were growing as the full orange moon crept into the dark purple sky, causing the evil angels on the buildings to reach out for her. She had been sitting there for a long time, as she tried to keep her long red hair from tangling up; the steady rain turned it into a tangled curly mess. Her mother would not be pleased.

The tiny girl was having a hard day. Early in the morning, some strange men dressed in black came to her small house and put her mother into a pine box. The sound of the nails as they were pounded into the box would haunt the little girl for the rest of her life. Later, a man she never saw before came and took her from her home. She heard people say her mother was taken by yellow fever and that the man was her father, but she was not sure what it all meant. It was her so-called father who brought her to this place. He sat her down on the cold steps outside, told her to stay, and then went inside. The sun was up when he went in. Now it was dark and raining. She was shivering from the cold and damp. She wished her mother would come get her and take her home.

As the sun started peeking up over the horizon, her father came out of the building, grabbed her by the arm, dragged her into a large room, stood her up on a table, and said, "She is strong and can work hard. It should cover my bet." She looked around the smoky room filled with noisy men and ornately dressed women. There was a rancid stale smell in the air and some pungent odor she could not

5

identify. The room was full of smoke coming from the men's cigars. Smoke swirled and drifted up to her head, making her cough.

The six old men at the table looked her over. They poked and prodded. The one with crooked stained teeth lifted the edge of her skirt and looked under it. The men talked among themselves for a while and then sat back down.

A lady with a sparkly dress and a huge feather in her hair came over to the table. She was all painted up, and her mouth was firm, but her eyes showed a spark of kindness. She started yelling at the men. After what seemed like a long time, the lady sat down and put a lot of money on the table at the little girl's feet. The people around the table were doing something with cards, and some of them were looking her over. The men started yelling again as the lady showed three aces and two eights.

The girl's father stood, turned to her, and told her, "You belong to Kitty now. She won you fair and square." He lifted her off the table, tilted his hat to the fancy lady, and said, "As always a pleasure." And he left.

She ran after him crying. How was she to get home? How was her mother going to find her?

The Gambling House

The sparkly lady named Kitty took her by the hand and dragged her up a very large staircase, grumbling as they climbed. Kitty said, "I don't know what I am going to do with you. All I need is a little brat to put up with. I must get back downstairs. You already caused me trouble. I was supposed to be working tonight, not playing poker." She dragged the young girl over to a large closet and gave her a pillow and a blanket. Pushing her in, she said, "You stay in here tonight. Don't come out no matter what you hear and don't make any noise."

The closet door was closed, and she heard the footsteps of the lady as she hurried away. Alone, the small girl looked around the compact space. There were rafters above her. The walls were bare, and there were some clothes strewed about in the warm dark closet. The pillow smelled like roses, and a small light crept through the slits in the door, making her feel a little better. Everything was strange to her. She missed her own little bed. She missed her rag doll she named Anna. She missed her mother. She lay down, hugged the pillow, and cried herself to sleep.

Not much later, she was awakened by loud voices. A man was yelling. She did not understand what he was saying. She heard the man hitting the lady. She huddled in a ball and prayed for her mother to come. She hovered with her ears covered until she once again fell into a fitful sleep.

The girl was very hungry when she woke up. She had not eaten in a long while. Hearing the lady sobbing in the other room. Slowly, she opened the door. Lying on the big rumpled bed was the lady from the night before, bleeding. The child got a towel and water from the pitcher on the dresser and started cleaning up the blood.

Kitty woke. "We are in a fix, girl," she said. Taking the towel, she wiped the girl's face. "Looks like you had a bad night also. Let's get you some food, and we will talk."

The tiny girl ate little. She was hungry, but the food seemed to turn her stomach.

Kitty spoke softly, "We all work around here. You belong here now, so you will too. You're too young to work the floor, so we will have you clean the spittoons, ashtrays, and glasses and sweep the place. In return, you will eat a good meal and sleep in the crawl space between the rooms. It will not be so bad. I will help you fix it up. What's your name, girl?"

The little girl tried to be thankful, but she was still shivering from fright. In a wavering voice, she replied, "Amanda Ann Arness. Pleased to meet you, madam."

Kitty smiled and laughed just a little. "That is just too long. I will call you Mandy."

In the days to come, Mandy worked from sunup until sundown. It was hard work, but she kind of liked it. It kept her busy. It kept her from thinking about her little room at home and her mother, whom she missed. She watched, and she learned.

Kitty was nice to her. Every night before going to work, she would read Mandy a story about faraway places. She even taught her to read some words. She said someday they would go see the West, as there was money to be made in the West and no law dog to take all the profits away. Mandy did not know what that meant, but it sounded nice. Kitty always had Mandy say her prayers before bed: "Please, God, keep me safe and take care of my mother. Thank you." Then Kitty gave her some food to snack on and locked her in the crawl space. "You will be safe in here," she would say.

Mandy slowly adapted to this new life. She learned to keep out of the way, while doing her assigned tasks. She thrived; she grew. She stayed out of trouble, that is until one summer day when the sun was shining very hot. She had been dutifully doing her regular chores. Hearing the riverboats whistle nearby, and she yearned to see them. Tommy, a little black boy who worked at the gambling house cleaning at night when the place was full of old men, wanted to see the riverboats also. Both children were tempted. Mandy regretfully told him she could not go, for she had to clean the spittoons. He came up with the idea of tying all the spittoons together with twine and throwing them into the river. The water would clean them, and they could see the boats. It seemed like a good idea, so they gathered the spittoons and some twine, and off they went down to the river. They were having a good old time soaking up the sun and running on the bank while the spittoons soaked in the river. They laughed as insects buzzed by and the sound of waves from the river lapped at the bank. A very large riverboat chugged past them, blowing its whistle. Mandy felt happy and free for the first time since they put her mother in that box. The waves from the paddle wheel got stronger as the boat turned, and it started picking up a little speed. The spittoons bobbled up and down in the high waves, clanging against one another. The old twine that held them together broke loose. The spittoons floated out into the river. In a panic, Mandy tried to reach them with a stick but only managed to sink them into the muddy water. They were gone. What was she to do? She would be in big trouble if she went back without the spittoons.

Now all the big houses had a practice of putting their extra spittoons out in back. Looking for a way to keep out of trouble if she returned without the spittoons, the kids went to the back of all the houses, gathering up the extra spittoons. They then placed them in the main room of the gambling house, hoping no one would notice the difference. What the kids did not know was that each house had their name engraved on their copper spittoons.

Mandy was locked in the crawl space when she heard sounds of a big fight. Some men were yelling that Kitty stole their spittoons. A violent fight ensued. Mandy needed to tell them what happened, that it wasn't Kitty's fault. Mandy kicked at the wall, yelling at the top of her lungs, to no avail.

The next day, Kitty was sporting a black eye and had large red marks on her arms. In the back room, some men were putting chains on Tommy's legs. Mandy was guilt ridden and upset. She tearfully confessed to Kitty what had happened with the spittoons. Kitty said it did not matter; it was too late. The boy was already sold to pay for the spittoons. Mandy cried as Tommy was pulled out onto the street. The boy, Tommy, did not cry. He held his head high. Kitty was very angry and slapped Mandy. "You never cry. It is a sign of weakness. No matter what anyone does to you, you never cry." Mandy stored Kitty's words away in her heart and would use them the rest of her life.

Mandy was now given Tommy's duties to perform. She would no longer live in the upstairs crawl space. Kitty showed her to a cot shoved behind the bottles in the back corner of the storage room. This was where she now would be staying. Kitty smiled. "It is not so bad. We will fix it up."

As part of her new duties, Kitty instructed her to stand at the end of the bar while keeping out of the way. She was to keep an eye on the tables, and when an ashtray got filled, she was to go over and dump it into a bucket. Also, she was to take any spittoons that got filled out back to be cleaned in the morning. Mandy took up her position at seven thirty in the evening. At first, the job was not that bad. The men were happy, and it was kind of exciting. The main room was lit with large chandeliers made of crystal. The light given off by the candles in the chandeliers was reflected in the bottles behind the hard polished oak bar and copper rails. The tables were covered with green felt, and a tapestry of a Bengal tiger hung on the wall. There were several tables in the room. A silver faro card box sat on every table. A lady dealer worked from each of the tables. She was dressed in fancy clothes and feathers and was always smiling at the men at the table.

The first night did not go so well. Mandy fell asleep several times, and the bartender would poke her and point to a table. When the sun finally came up, the plain cot in the back storage room looked awfully good to her. Mandy's workday was not over yet. Kitty called her in front of her and asked to recount what she saw the night before. Mandy did not remember anything. Kitty was not pleased by this. "Tomorrow night, I expect you to watch everything and report in the morning." Mandy was also not allowed to go to sleep until the night's take was totaled and entered into the books. Back in the dark cold storage room, Mandy slipped several pennies given to her as tips into the loose threads of her pillow. As she saved the pennies, she wondered how many pennies she would need to buy Tommy back.

Mandy would never see Tommy again, but she would never forget him. Whenever she saw Black men in chains being beaten in the street, she would pray that never happened to Tommy, but knew it probably had. She would often cry for him and his fate while in the privacy of her cot.

In the months to come, Mandy noticed and studied everything that happened in the main room. She blended into the background but was a keen observer. She learned that faro was played with thirteen cards, ace through king. The suit did not matter; only face value counted. The dealer dealt two cards from a deck of fifty-two. The object was to predict which card would come up next. The first card would win for the dealer. The second for the player. Winning or losing occurred when cards turned up by the banker matched those already exposed. Mandy paid close attention and soon realized the house could not win at this game. She began to wonder where the money was being made.

She noticed the lady dealers would take the winners of the games upstairs to celebrate after the table closed. Mandy also realized the free champagne given to the men when they entered the house was seldom drank. The men would instead pay a large price for whiskey that made them act silly. A man not drinking was not desirable, as he had his wits about him when he played the games. Within a short time, Mandy could report on who was in the house, what game they played, whether they won or lost, and if they were cheating and how. Kitty was pleased. Then she instructed her to listen to everything in the room, to hear every conversation. This skill was very hard to master as English, Spanish, French, and Cajun were all spoken in the house. But Mandy worked at learning some of the languages.

Over time, Mandy also learned to do hair, makeup, nails and to sew for the ladies. As time went by and she got older, Mandy was put in charge of the ladies of the house wardrobe. This was in addition to carrying water upstairs for the girls' baths, cleaning ashtrays, and watching the main room. About this time, Mandy started to develop into a young lady. She was not plain to look at but instead had a sweet pretty face and glorious red hair. A smattering of freckles was dusted across her cheekbones, and her lips were full with a slight curve.

Becoming a Dealer

Things were going okay until one fateful night. Mandy was standing in her usual place at the end of the bar, watching a fancy dandy lose. There was nothing unusual that Mandy could discern. The man was drinking very heavily and losing abundantly. Mandy knew this was a portent of trouble but was totally shaken and unprepared when the man suddenly pulled out a big gun and shot Mary, the dealer, right in her face. Connie, the floor boss, quickly responded by pulling out her own weapon and shooting the man dead. Everything happened so quickly. The table was closed. Mary was carried upstairs. It was a gruesome scene with blood everywhere and the metallic smell of the blood permeating the air. Mandy was handed a wooden bucket and rags and told to clean the blood spatters off the wall, table, and floor. She did this disgusting job quickly, trying not to throw up or cry. Throughout it all, she was amazed that the other tables never stopped but carried on business as usual.

After the body of the dead man had been removed from the premises and she managed to get the table sufficiently cleaned up, she was taken upstairs and given the job of nursing the critically ill Mary. Mary had been a beautiful woman, with warm brown eyes and a quick smile. The bullet had horribly ripped her face apart. The damage was irreparable. In extreme pain, she hovered between life and death for days. In between jobs, the other ladies of the gambling house would stop in to check on Mary. Appalled, they would make comments, like "It would be better if she dies. If she lives, she will surely starve."

Mary took almost two agonizing weeks to die. When she finally did, men in black coats with black top hats came, put her in a pine box, and carried her out. Afterward, Kitty brought Mandy one of

Mary's dresses. She told her to alter the dress and fix it up for herself to wear. Mandy felt strange and reluctant about the dress but did as she was told. That night, Mandy dealt at Mary's table, wearing the altered fancy dress that left her shoulders bare. The fancy dress made her look older than her tender years.

Regarding being a dealer, Kitty told her, "The table has to make a profit. Mr. Jones, who owns the house on paper, will not tolerate a loss." Kitty had won the house in a poker game, but because a woman could not legally own property, Mr. Jones was the public owner. He got free use of the house. And he enjoyed handing out punishment when the mood suited him, mostly with the girls upstairs.

The first night, Mandy's table made a profit only because the bartender slipped extra money into the till for her. However, the second night as a dealer, Mandy was losing money. She lost $500 by midnight when she was removed from the table and taken to Kitty's room. Kitty grimaced and looked up from her dressing table. "I told you we cannot tolerate a loss. The house cannot win at faro unless you get creative."

Mandy wanted to say something in her defense. Before she could utter a word, Mr. Jones came, angrily striding into the room. With a pompous stance, he stopped before Mandy. "Well, missy, you cost me $500 tonight. How do you figure on making it up?" Looking the young beautiful redhead up one side and down the other, he smiled. "You have developed into a good-looking woman," he said with a leer of anticipation.

Kitty immediately jumped up. She protested, "No! She is too young. I don't want her doing that."

Mr. Jones then backhanded Kitty, sending her crashing to the floor. Mandy was too frightened to move. Mr. Jones turned to Kitty where she sat crumpled on the floor and snarled, "You want to take what I should do to her?"

Kitty awkwardly stood up. Without taking her eyes off Mr. Jones, she said to Mandy, "Get out of here, Mandy. Get out!"

Mr. Jones unbuckled and took off his belt. Slapping it menacingly in his hand, he said, "I am going to enjoy this."

Kitty again yelled, "Get out, Mandy!"

A traumatized Mandy turned and started running out the door and down the stairs out into the street. She did not feel the cold of the night on her bare shoulders as she sprinted down Canal Street. She ran blindly until her side hurt and her breath was labored. She finally stopped running when she reached the steep grassy bank of the Mississippi River.

Mandy was drawn to the edge of the raging river. Its waves seemed to call to her, "Jump, jump." With each wave, it called louder until she covered her ears to keep the river out. Her face was ashen, and her body trembled. Her breath was shallow, and her eyes were a bit wild. Her red hair had come down from its clip and brushed over her shoulders. She tried to keep the taunting sound of the river out of her head.

"Are you okay?" a soft masculine voice asked. "The river is too cold to swim in at night, you know."

Mandy turned to see a very handsome man standing behind her on the grassy bank. He was over six feet tall, with clear blue eyes, thick brown hair, a handsome face, and a nice smile. He proceeded to take off his coat and put it around her shoulders, warming her against the cool night air.

The moonlight reflected in the waves of the river as the two talked. The man walked her away from the river's edge and bought her coffee at a local café. Then he patiently walked her back to the gambling house. Mandy was embarrassed for the first time about working in the house. However, this man did not seem to be bothered by it. He looked at her earnestly and said, "My name is James." He asked her to meet him by the river the next afternoon. Mandy regretfully told him she did not think she could get away. He then kissed her softly on the palm of her hand. "I will be by the river most days. Perhaps I will see you again if fate allows."

Growing Up

When a subdued Mandy entered the gambling house, the bartender handed her a basin full of water. "I am glad you are back. It's about time. I have been covering for you. Take this up to Kitty."

Mandy was afraid and would have taken off running, but she had no place else to go. So taking the basin, up the stairs she went on unsteady legs. She was fearful of what she might find. She tepidly opened the door and went into Kitty's room. Kitty was sitting on the side of the rumpled bed wearing a loose nightshirt. Her hair was down loose around her shoulders. Mandy was relieved when she saw no overt signs of Kitty being beaten up.

Kitty sighed and said, "Put the water over by the table and come sit with me."

In a small voice, Mandy asked, "Did he hurt you?"

Kitty replied, "Nothing I can't handle. I know life has been hard for you. I have been thinking. I am going to take you off the faro table. We are going to offer another game called poker. They play it a lot in the West. I think you will be good at it. I want you to learn it well."

Mandy looked at Kitty with promise in her eyes. "I will. Can we go to the West?"

Kitty said, "Someday. You and I will take that stagecoach and ride to a better future."

Just then the door flew open and hit the wall with a loud bang. It was an angry Mr. Jones who stood menacingly in the doorway. "So there you are. Thought you could get away, did you?" He grabbed Mandy by the hair, tugged and threw her down on the rumpled bed, and jumped on top of her.

Kitty yelled, "No! Get off her. No!" Kitty launched herself onto his back, circling her hands around his head and sticking her fingers in his eyes. He was strong and easily threw her off him. She landed with a thud across the room.

"So you did not get enough last night," he said as he got off the bed, leaving a frightened Mandy, and moved stealthily toward Kitty. His face was red; his eyes were ice-cold and hard, and a vein was bulging on his forehead. The grotesque look on his face was maniacal. He loomed over Kitty. "I am going to hurt you good so you won't forget this time!" he yelled.

As he grabbed Kitty by the neck, Mandy reached over and grabbed the silver letter opener from the top of the oak dresser. Without any forethought, she ran up behind him and plunged the letter opener into Mr. Jones' back. He turned in a rage and struck Mandy, sending her flying across the room. Blood trickled from the corner of her mouth. Before he could go after her further, Kitty jumped on him, hitting him on the head. Together they fell to the floor, with Kitty landing on top. Kitty started hitting his head against the floor. He rolled over on top of her and began punching Kitty in the face. The crack of the punches was nauseating, and Kitty moaned. That's when Mandy stabbed him again. She pulled out the letter opener and stabbed him once more for Kitty and once for Mary. She stabbed him for Tommy. Then when he rolled over with his back on the bedroom floor, she sunk the letter opener deep into his chest to pay him for what he was going to do to her—so deep she could not pull it back out. She was hysterical, and hot tears ran down her face.

Kitty grabbed her and pulled her over into a corner. Her arms wrapped around Mandy's trembling shoulders. Running one of her hands down Mandy's disheveled hair, she pulled Mandy into a comforting hug. "He is dead," she said softly. "We must get hold of ourselves." She wrapped her protective arms around the young girl to comfort her and give her strength. "We have many things to do. You must calm yourself. We are in big trouble." Mandy was covered head to toe with Mr. Jones' warm, sticky blood. Kitty stood and went over to retrieve the water basin. "Take off your clothes. Hurry! Wash your face and hands." Mandy did as she was told, discarding her soiled dress in a heap in the corner. She then wrapped herself in a robe that had been thrown over the back of a chair. Kitty pulled the goose-feather-filled mattress off the bed, rolled Mr. Jones up in it, and tied it with belts and ribbons. "Go get Connie while I am cleaning up." Connie was the watcher and floor boss at the gambling house. "Only Connie, no one else."

Kitty was mopping up the blood-soaked floor when Mandy and Connie entered the room.

Connie took in the scene. "This is big trouble," Connie announced as she helped Kitty move the body over to the window. "What happened?" Connie asked.

Kitty replied, "Does it matter?"

Connie said, "Not to me. Come with me, Mandy."

Mandy quickly put on street clothes and followed Connie out of the gambling house. With purpose, Connie calmly walked a few blocks to the barrel maker. She shopped for just the right barrel, the way Kitty shopped for a bolt of cloth, inspecting each one. The barrel maker kept trying to sell her a whiskey barrel. Connie did not want this because they were lined with pitch and made of thicker and choicer wood. She explained to Mandy the size of the barrels varied, but likely, most of the barrels were of a size known as tierce or about forty-two gallons—the size of a barrel of petroleum or salt. She looked at meat, apple, nail, oil, and salt barrels before deciding on a potato barrel. It was not lined and had one broken wooden plank along the long part of the barrel. The barrel maker hesitated. He did not want to sell it. He had too much pride in his craft to sell a defective barrel. But Connie told him it was going to be used to store wire and therefore did not need to be of first quality. He gave her the barrel.

Next, she bought some lime. She gathered up a whiskey wagon and some rope. They put the barrel and other supplies on the wagon box and took through town to the back of the gambling house. There, they parked it under Kitty's window. Then they made their way up to the room.

Mandy hesitantly asked, "Shouldn't we wait until dark?"

Connie said, "After dark, this place will be crawling with people. We need to do this now. No one will notice us." She tied the rope securely around Mr. Jones' torso, under his arms. So midday in plain sight of everyone who cared to look, the three women lowered Mr. Jones, wrapped in a sheet, out the window. His weight got the best of them, and the rope slipped. Mr. Jones fell, landing half in and half out of the barrel below. Connie and Mandy ran down the back stairs. They pushed on Mr. Jones with all their might until he was stuffed in the barrel. Connie dumped the lime in over the body, then nailed the lid of the barrel shut.

While Kitty worked putting everything back to order at the gambling house, Mandy and Connie together pulled the wagon through the public streets. Mandy feared that, any moment, Mr. Jones would jump out of the barrel and grab her. She also worried someone might stop them and want to know what they had in the barrel. But fortunately, no one even gave them a second glance. Once they got to the Mississippi River, they heaved the barrel off the wagon and rolled it out to sea.

That should have been the end of it, but the darn thing floated! Connie threw rocks at it. That just made it bobble around. They tried to think what to do next. A boat went past the barrel. The barrel got caught in the wake and floated downstream. "Oh well," Connie said, "the lime should eat his features. Even if someone opens it, it is unlikely they will trace it back to us."

Back in Kitty's room after getting cleaned up, Connie took Mandy by the shoulders. She admonished, "You must never ever speak of this. Now get dressed, go downstairs, and smile."

As Mandy descended the front staircase, she saw Kitty smiling and laughing as if nothing had happened. As the night wore on, Mandy was surprised that no one seemed to even miss Mr. Jones. They were all better off without him.

The gambling house continued to remain in his name until 1862 when the Homestead Act made it easier for single women to claim land in their own name.

The Riverboat

Kitty desperately wanted to get Mandy out of New Orleans. Mandy, though still very young, was becoming more beautiful and attracting attention. Not only was she shapely, her skin was flawless. So unlike the other girls, she had no need for heavy makeup. Men did not realize how young she really was.

Kitty procured a job on a riverboat and took six girls with her. Mandy was glad to be one of them. She remembered her previous fascination with the riverboats on the Mississippi River. The ship was made of wood with a length nearly 150 feet and 60 feet wide and drawing only about 1 to 5 feet of water when loaded. The boat was quite ornate with wooden trim, velvet plush chairs, and gilt edging. It had a large decorative staircase, fancy galleys, and several lucrative parlors. It ran by woodburning boilers that were forward center to distribute weight. The engines were also located midship because this particular riverboat was a side-wheeler. It was a grand sight. The girls' shared cabin was tucked away on the second deck.

It was a grand adventure. Mandy was dreaming of seeing the wonderful things she had never before seen and meeting different people than the usual older gamblers. The first day was exciting as Mandy was taken in by the beauty, the newness, and the grandeur of it all. She was given to wear a brightly colored ruffled skirt that was scandalously short—knee-length. Under the bell shape was a colorfully hued petticoat that barely reached her kid boots and was adorned with tassels. Her arms and shoulders were bare, the bodice cut low over her bosoms. The dress was decorated with sequins and fringe. She was given net stockings and decorative garters to hold them up. Her face was painted, and feathers adorned her hair.

Her job was to sing for the men, dance with them, and talk to them—inducing them into buying drinks and patronizing the games. That was when she was not occupied dealing cards. She was strictly told the house does not lose. Mandy therefore learned to lower her shoulder in a sultry manner as she dealt cards, allowing the drunken men a free look. This would distract most of the gamblers, allowing her to switch cards at her will. She worked as a dealer from noon till four. After that, she would take her place in the chorus line. The lively show would last an hour. Mandy then had a half hour to herself to freshen up and return to the floor until the next dance four hours later. This would go on until seven in the morning. Mandy would then eat and try to get some sleep. Even then, she was often called upon when needed to replace another dealer who was called away for other duties. It was a hard, long, tiring work.

On the riverboat, her diet was mostly boiled eggs and watered-down tea. This bland fare would actually remain her staple meal for years to come. She kind of liked the fast pace and all the glamour on the riverboat for the first three days. By then she was exhausted and just wanted to go to bed, pull the covers over her head, and sleep.

Mandy got used to the fast-paced living on the riverboat. In essence, she learned control and how to maintain a calm demeanor. She perfected flirting with the customers without giving of herself. She knew the men found her attractive.

One day after she had been working on the riverboat for a while, she was sitting on a man's lap, letting him lick her neck at two o'clock in the morning. Suddenly, a violent explosion shook the vessel and tossed her up against the wall. Holding her head where it smashed against the wall, she glanced over to see the man she was just sitting on lying lifeless on the floor. His vacant eyes were staring up at the ornate ceiling. She got to her feet and quickly ran to find Kitty. When she got to their cabin on the second floor, all the girls were looking for Kitty to find out what they should do. The boat was pitching in an odd manner. Among the confusion and shouts on the boat, they learned that a poorly repaired boiler had exploded, causing severe damage.

Two of the other boilers then exploded in rapid succession, and a fire began licking its way through midship. The two smokestacks thunderously collapsed and fell onto the boat, crushing the top deck and killing many instantly. Panicked chaos ensued. Fleeing passengers were pushing and shoving in an attempt to reach safety. Those who survived and were able to move began to jump into the river below in their panic. Kitty opened her cabin door to see what was happening and assess their best course of action. She was immersed in a cloud of steam. She quickly slammed the door shut tight. She pulled life belts from under the bed and put them on herself and Mandy, opened the door again, and rushed the girls to the stern of the rocking boat. They had to climb across overturned chairs and bodies on deck. There they climbed down a secured rope to the lower deck. Kitty and the girls then jumped into the freezing water. Mandy, however, held back in terror. She was reluctant to go into the water as she had not been swimming in many years. Surely, she would go under and drown. But fear of the encroaching fire finally caused her to react and follow the others into the river below. When she hit the cold water, she discovered her life preserver had been fastened incorrectly, and she lost it as it was torn from her body. But Mandy was a fighter and not ready to give up. She managed to grab onto the rudder that was close by. By now, Mandy was almost hysterical. Then, in horror, she saw Kitty and the girls drift away and disappear into the current. They were soon lost from sight.

The spreading fire began to engulf the rudder to which she held. She released her grip to avoid the encroaching flames and managed to grab onto a small nearby board. She watched the flaming remains of the riverboat lighting up the night sky as she floated away. The river was high, cold, flowing fast, and crowded with the dead, dying, drowning, and barely floating men. The boat was now entirely engulfed in flames, casting a beacon of light on the river that could be seen from a great distance. Some of the survivors floating in the muddy water began to sing marching tunes while holding on to their driftwood rafts. Others joined in. This was to give themselves courage and the strength to endure.

After floating desolately among the chaos for a while, Mandy felt someone grab her by her hair and the belt of her dress. The man plucked her dripping from the cold river, dropping her into the bottom of a small boat. Before she could get her breath, the man yelled at her to help the others. Mandy managed to hang near the edge of the wooden boat and pull three more from the high muddy water. She then grabbed hold of a small child who was floating by on one side.

"Drop her!" the man yelled. "We have no room for the dead."

In shock, not realizing the child was dead, Mandy still kept hold of her until someone hit her. She let go, and the child drifted off, bobbing like a bottle in the murky water. Mandy fell back into the bottom of the boat and was soon covered by others who had been pulled out of the river.

"We have to make for shore now! We cannot hold any more!" someone yelled.

They started paddling toward shore, but the small overloaded fishing boat started taking on water. A man handed Mandy his hat, and as he paddled, she bailed water as fast as she could. They got closer to the bank. But despite their best efforts, they did not make it the whole way, and the boat sank in about four feet of water.

The Boyfriend

Mandy wearily climbed out onto the bank, wet and exhausted from trudging through the muddy water with her water-soddened skirt pulling her down. Her arms ached from hoisting other weighted people into the small boat. Her whole body ached from the ordeal of escaping the flaming riverboat. Even her mind was tired from the overload of adrenaline that had now dissipated. One of the men from the boat was concerned and asked if she was all right. With a harried look on her face, she exclaimed, "I need to find my friends!"

There seemed to be people scattered everywhere. Some were badly burned and pitifully begging for someone to help them. Heartbreaking as it was, Mandy tried not to look at them, for there was no help she could give them.

Mandy and the man who rescued her carefully walked the bank, scanning the crowd of bedraggled people but not seeing anyone they knew. Finally, without hope, they sat on a deserted bench farther up the bank, and the man checked his pocket. "Would you like a cup of coffee? You are shivering. Maybe it will warm you some." Mandy agreed.

They went to a small restaurant about a block away, but the people at the eating establishment refused to serve Mandy because her dress was unsuitable. Not because it was wet and water stained but because they recognized it for the saloon-gal dress that it was. Mandy resignedly turned around and walked back outside, her bare shoulders slumped. She was used to this treatment and just too tired to fight anyone about anything. The man stayed behind, bought them both coffee, and brought it outside. He handed her the hot aromatic brew and had her sit down again on the bench. The man finally introduced himself as Bill Inking. He was about fifteen years older than Mandy, handsome, well-mannered, and well-dressed.

Dawn broke over the land. Mandy again searched for her friends, to no avail. There was nowhere for them to go in this small town. She did not belong here. She knew it, and the town knew it. Mandy and the man called Bill Inking, having no ready money, set out to walk back to New Orleans. The weeks to come were hard ones. Along the way, they would meet people who refused to help them or associate with them because of Mandy's attire. Bill solved this dilemma by stealing an ordinary dress from a clothesline. After Mandy changed her clothes, they were able to hitch a ride on a cotton wagon.

After days of hitching rides, walking dusty roads together, and nights spent under a starlit sky, Mandy fell madly in love with the man who rescued her. She had never been in love before. It was that kind of love that was deaf, dumb, blind, and wonderful. When he took her hand, she would get goose bumps. When he whispered in her ear, her heart skipped a beat. She gave everything to him, gave too much. She didn't care how much she hurt. She just wanted to please him.

In years to come, she would look back at this time and knew it was worth it all. She never forgot how she felt that first wonderful year before life and reality took them astray. Although only thirteen, Mandy's life had made her old for her years. She looked and acted more mature than her tender age. Yet in some ways, she was still naive, and she had no idea how to deal with her first love. Bill was her hero who pulled her from death's hand in the freezing water. She worshipped him for that. He was the only one willing to help her after she got on dry land.

When the lights of New Orleans finally came into view, Mandy was sad and weary. The trip had been long and arduous. She had to go days without food. Drinking water was obtained from the river or ditches, and the nights were cold as they spent them on the hard packed ground. But New Orleans meant coming to terms with Kitty's and the girls' deaths. She would never forget seeing their ravaged faces as they floated away out of sight in the churning river. Mandy also wondered if Connie had taken over the gambling house with Kitty now gone. Would she welcome her? Would she let Mandy work there?

Seeing the city of New Orleans was bittersweet. Although her goal throughout the journey had been to get back to New Orleans, Mandy began to realize there was nothing left there for her. No welcome face for her. She thought being back would bring happiness. It didn't, although she felt the comfort of being someplace familiar. Memories flowed back to her. She thought of Tommy and the spittoons, Mr. Jones in the barrel floating off to sea, and Kitty and her closet. The most bittersweet thoughts were of her mother reading her stories in her soft bed and, later, that pine box that took her away. She was surprised at how the thoughts of the nice young man she met on the riverbank the night Mr. Jones died filled her with warmth and peace.

At the edge of town, Bill sensed her hesitation. "Life is best faced head-on. I have a room above the King's saloon. If you find you have no place to go, you can stay with me," he said.

Mandy had some romantic notions dancing in her head about living with Bill. Part of her wished she would not have a job and would have to take him up on his offer.

They turned the corner, and there it was—the gambling house. It was gorgeous, standing strong against the dark storm-ridden sky. Ordinary in its architecture yet delightfully elegant. Mandy was flooded with great happiness and, at the same time, overwhelming sadness.

Upon entering the gambling house, Mandy was overjoyed to find that all the girls had survived the raging river. It was a miracle. Kitty herself was standing regally on the stairs. When she saw Mandy, she could not believe it. The two women ran into each other's arms. Kitty allowed a single tear to sneak down her face.

The happy reunion was short-lived when Mandy introduced Bill to Kitty. Kitty recognized Bill for what he was with just one look. When she saw the spark in Mandy's eyes, she hoped she was wrong. Kitty wanted to know everything about Mandy's survival and how she managed to make it home. Mandy explained how great a hero Bill was. Kitty said nothing, only smiled that saloon-gal smile. Mandy found this troubling.

Mandy's mood turned to sadness as she related an incident during the return trip regarding a group of slaves that were taking produce to market. Mandy, meaning no harm, said hello to one of the men as they passed.

The overseer came running over and beat the man with a whip. He kept yelling, "I'll teach you not to look at a white woman!" Mandy tried to explain, but the overseer yelled at Bill, "Control your woman! If she were mine, I would lay the whip against her back for not having on her hat and gloves! It is shameful!"

Bill pulled Mandy away from the overseer. "When I get you home, you will answer for this!" he yelled at her. Once they got out of earshot, Bill explained that the overseer was within his rights to have beaten Mandy and to have the Negro killed.

Mandy asked Kitty if Bill was right. Kitty explained that the plantation owner did have the right to have Mandy beaten if she was enticing a Negro.

Mandy stated, "I only said hello."

Kitty went on to say, "Negros who talk to or even look at a White woman could legally be killed at the discretion of the owner. The plantation owner owned the Negro's life."

Mandy thought this over with a sense of dread. Then she admitted to Kitty that she had a sum of money saved and hidden in her room. "Can we buy Tommy back?" Unnoticed to her, Bill's ears perked up when Mandy mentioned money.

Kitty said, "Tommy was sold to a broker. The broker usually resells his lot at the common market. The courthouse may have a record of the sale, but a lot of plantation owners change the name of their slaves. We may not be able to find him."

Mandy was distraught at this news, but she and Kitty took a trip to the courthouse and found the census record of the sale at the gambling house. The record stated Tommy and eight other seven-year-old boys were sold at the common market. There was a long list of buyers that day. There was no way to tell to which owner he had been sold.

Kitty put a comforting hand on Mandy's slumped shoulder. "I am truly sorry. Tommy is lost. Mr. Jones made the sale. I could not stop him."

Mandy knew Mr. Jones had controlled the house, but she could not, would not, ever forgive Kitty.

Bill saw his opportunity and used this to drive a wedge between the two women. He would visit Mandy and casually drop references about Tommy's sale into the conversation. He would sway the conversation in such a way as to make Kitty's actions appear callous. Within a week, he had both Mandy's penny jar and her week's wages in his possession. Kitty tried, in a rational way, to explain to her how an older man could take advantage of a young girl, but Mandy was too much in love with Bill to hear.

One night soon after, Bill asked Mandy to marry him. Mandy's heart soared with happiness. She was on cloud nine. They walked down by the river hand in hand. She let Bill kiss her. It was a soft kiss that instilled a strange longing unknown to her. Bill pressed his advantage. There under the shade of a weeping willow, the thirty-five-year-old man took the thirteen-year-old girl. Afterward, Bill gently caressed her cheek and said they should move in together in order to save money for their future.

Sex and Money

The room Bill had rented was small, had no windows, and smelled like the downstairs bar. It was sparsely furnished and needed to be painted. Mandy loved it. It was the first time in her life she had a place of her own. The one-room apartment had a water room and a big bed, but not much else. Mandy was happy as a lark. For the first time in years, she had a real bed. Mandy was happy. Kitty, who disapproved of the arrangement, gave her linens to fix up the drab room. Bill did not like Kitty coming over and made Mandy stop inviting her. In addition to her job at the gambling house, Bill got Mandy a second job in the saloon downstairs. He told her he would keep the money she earned and save it for their future. Mandy thought that was sensible. Although Mandy was now working sixteen hours a day, she had no money as she gave it all to Bill.

Mandy finally got a day off from both jobs. She felt free. She was lighthearted and happily skipped as she made her way through the dark streets of New Orleans. She stopped on a footbridge to look at some ducks. Hoping to get some sleep before the most wonderful man in the world made it home, she started to run. Getting home, Mandy was surprised to find a huge older guy waiting inside their room. Before she could ask what he was doing there, he grabbed her with his beefy hands and roughly threw her down on the bed. He then ripped her dress off and violently raped her. She struggled, but he overpowered her. When he was done, he rolled off and said, "I have to give Bill credit. He sure can pick them."

Mandy was in shock. At first, she did not believe it. *No, he couldn't have!* Then when Bill came in to collect the money, her tender heart was irreparably broken into a million pieces. She just wanted to curl up and die.

Bill came over to her after the man left. "Now that was not so bad. You do three more and I will have the stakes I need to get into a game tonight. I will win enough for us to get married."

Mandy now knew Kitty was right when she tried to warn her. But what was she to do? Kitty no longer acknowledged her after she stopped associating with her at Bill's request. She had no one to turn to.

Bill no longer allowed Mandy to work outside the apartment. In fact, he did not want her leaving the room at all. The few times she tried, he beat her unmercifully. He set up the liaisons. He always took the money yet never had any to buy food or wood for heat.

It did not take long for Kitty to find out what was going on. It just so happened Kitty was good friends with the commanding officer of the Guard Deville City Watch, a militia group. He had Bill arrested for loitering and taken to the local stockade. Once locked up, Kitty came waltzing in, signaling the man in the cell with Bill. At her signal, the large man grabbed Bill by the back of the neck and stuffed his face between the bars. Kitty approached his flushed face and said in a soft voice, "You have two choices. One, you can stay in New Orleans, in which case I will have to feed you to the fish. Or you can leave and never come back. Either way, you will have no more to do with Mandy."

Bill blustered and yelled, "She is my property!"

Kitty grabbed Bill's nose like a vise and pulled it through the cold metal bars. "You will have no more to do with Mandy, or you will swim with the fish." To drive her message home, Kitty signaled the other man in the cell, who obligingly beat Bill to a pulp.

Unknowing what was happening, Mandy waited alone in the apartment. No one came, and she was afraid to leave. She feared the knock on the door yet yearned for someone to come. Bill had been gone for three days. Food was running out. Although frightened, she finally worked up the nerve to leave the apartment with no money. She timidly opened the door and descended the steps. Seeing no one she knew, she continued on until she got to the gambling house. Mandy had gone to Kitty.

Kitty met her on the staircase. Mandy looked thin and ravaged. Her hair was matted in places, nails cracked and short, her dress dirty, and the lace torn. But worse was the hollow, defeated look in Mandy's blue eyes. Kitty just stood there and made Mandy ask for help. When she did, Kitty passed Mandy, head held high. "So you want to work for me. I don't think I need anyone just now. I have all the dealers I need." Mandy was close to tears. She had no money and nowhere to go. She was destitute. She stood humbly with her head downcast. Kitty softened. "I need someone to clean the spittoons. You want the job?" Mandy gratefully took the job but, even then, feared what Bill would do to her when he found her.

Kitty did not make the next month easy for Mandy. She was once again sleeping on the cot in the back, cleaning spittoon, polishing the bar, dumping ashtrays, and sweeping floors. Mandy did not ask for money, and Kitty offered none. Mandy ate leftovers from the free lunch table and boiled eggs.

By the end of the next month, Mandy began to relax. She no longer feared Bill coming after her. She gained strength in her mind and body. The haunted look in her eyes was gone. Kitty watched her blossom and regain her confidence. She slowly gave Mandy the watching job. Finally, Mandy advanced to the job as poker dealer and was making a reasonable wage. Every day men requested Mandy's time.

Becoming a Working Gal

One day, Mandy was called to Kitty's office. Kitty offered her a room upstairs. Mandy now knew what that meant. Kitty complimented her by saying, "With your appealing looks, you would make a lot of money upstairs. Women must strive to make their money when they are young. The world will throw you away without a second thought when you get old. So now, you should save as much money as you can. I will not ask you to entertain anyone you do not wish to. You have that freedom to reject a customer. You will be charged a daily rate for the room, and the house gets twenty-five percent of the take. It will take accommodating about five men a month before you make any money. I think you will find this standard. In return, you get the room. I will introduce you to some gentlemen buyers, and you get protection."

And so Mandy became a working gal. That was the way it was. She was given a nice but modest room on the upper floor. It had a large comfortable bed, a small armoire, a chair, and a small closet space. Mandy was happy there and had a sense of belonging.

Mandy was soon making money hand over fist. She was very sought-after. The men Kitty introduced to her were rich. For the most part, they were easy to deal with—not like the brutes Bill brought home. In fact, none of the men got rough with Mandy, for that would cause them to be asked to leave and not return.

One night, Mandy was losing badly to a man who showed an interest in going upstairs with her. Without first getting Kitty's approval, Mandy closed her table and took the man, his winnings, and a bottle upstairs. Once behind the door in her room, the man's demeanor drastically changed. He restrained her, gagged her, bent her over the bed, pulled up her dress, and began beating her with his belt. Then he tied her to the bed face up. Using a sharp knife, he cut her dress off, throwing the scraps of the ruined dress onto the floor. Using a candle, he dripped hot wax on her as his eyes lit up in glee. He had sex with her and rested on her. She was in agony but still gagged and tied, so she was unable to get away. He then beat her again, saying he was going to drive the devil from her soul. He heated coins until they were red-hot and then placed them on her, burning the delicate skin of her chest. Using the last of her reserve, she finally was able to work the gag loose and yell for help. Kitty heard the cries for help and came running. She burst into the room, grabbed the man, and threw him out.

A few days later as she was recovering, Mandy read in the newspaper the wicked man was found beaten to death in the street. Mandy asked Kitty about it. All Kitty said was "A man like that has many enemies. It was not surprising he would end like that. By the way, you should raise your price." Soon, Mandy became the highest-paid woman in New Orleans. She had her own group of clients—high rollers every one. And she used a lot more care in who she took as customers.

Kitty and Mandy were shopping for new hats when they got the word Lawrence, Kansas, had been ransacked. It meant little to them. One of Kitty's strict rules was that no one affiliated with her saloon should get involved in politics. She welcomed the men who worked under French, Spanish, English, and even Confederate flags. She did not discriminate. Her rule was that if a man had paper money, that was good. Coins were better. Gold? Come on in. Everyone could feel the wave of change that was upon them. It was hard not to be sucked into a political conversation.

The city was a great place to be in the year 1855. A large cotton crop brought riches to everyone. Money was spent freely. The gambling house benefited from out-of-town buyers. It was a time for everyone to celebrate.

Sickness, Punishment, and Escape

Unfortunately, the bumper crop of cotton also had a residual effect which brought lots of mosquitoes that swarmed the city. In addition, poor sanitation led to an outbreak of cholera. Being uninformed in such matters, people mistakenly thought that whiskey was a cure for cholera. Believing this, they flocked to the bar. Even Kitty ordered all her girls to drink a dose of strong whiskey every morning.

As debilitating as the cholera was, it was ultimately the American plague that rocked the gambling house. Yellow fever. Everyone was coming down sick. Men stopped coming in to patronize the saloon because a physician posted a yellow flag on the front door. Fear expanded rapidly. The government placed a large oil barrel in front of the house because yellow fever was thought to be airborne. The smoke from the burning oil was to keep down the spread of the disease. The gambling house was filled with smelly black smoke, and an oily soot covered everything. The windows of the house rattled and broke as the government fired off cannons to drive the sickness out of the air. It was a terrible time for everyone. Animals also caught the disease and died; their decomposing carcasses littered the streets. Everyone was afraid to touch them for fear of catching the disease, so the bodies remained there. The putrid odor was almost unbearable. A curfew was put into effect. This essentially put the gambling house out of business.

Kitty was still entertaining the French soldiers who were unaffected by the curfew and could walk through the town freely. But the French soldiers then also became sick. Many died. Kitty and the gambling house were blamed. She was arrested and charged with treason because she entertained men who openly worked under the Confederate flag. She was taken away and placed in the city jail.

With no one to keep order, the gambling house was ransacked, then set on fire. Seeing the flames, Mandy ran into the burning building, up to the second floor, and grabbed the lockbox she had hidden there. She was then trapped, as the fire consumed the front staircase. Moving swiftly through the crawl space, she jumped out onto Connie's bed in the next room. She saw two street dresses. Grabbing them, she then jumped out the back window with the dresses and the lockbox, just barely making her escape.

Having escaped, Mandy was able to use the money from the lockbox to buy passage on a riverboat leaving New Orleans after being cleared from quarantine. After purchasing her ticket, she then went to the jail and paid a heavy price, both personal and monetary, to the guards to let Kitty out. The guards, having been paid, turned a blind eye as Kitty made her escape. The riverboat was blowing its horn as the two women ran down Canal Street.

All at once, Kitty stopped on the cobblestone street. "We cannot leave yet," she said.

Mandy tried to tug her along while yelling, "We have to catch that boat!"

Kitty held back, stooped, and started gathering wildflowers by the roadside. "You follow me. We won't be long," she said as she ran into Lafayette Cemetery.

Mandy did not like cemeteries. She was frightened of the angels and gargoyles. Kitty ran past the ornate ironwork, past the Greek revival-style tombs and stopped in front of a small plain tomb. Mandy read the inscription—Elizabeth Ann Arness. "Mother?" She looked over at Kitty.

Kitty removed the old dried flowers from the grave. "I found it years ago. I've been putting flowers on it to thank her for you, my child. But you are going away for a long time. Now you will say goodbye. I will wait over there." Kitty handed her some flowers, then went over to stand by a small grave of a child.

Mandy was stunned and started to cry. "Mommy, I am sorry I have been so mad at you. I know you did not want to leave me. Kitty has been good to me. She took good care of me."

The boat gave three small blasts on its horn. Kitty ran up to Mandy. "We've got to go!"

Mandy hastily put the flowers down. "Bye, Mommy. I miss you every day."

They ran for the boat. It was still loading large bales of cotton. Mandy and Kitty walked up the dock. At an opportune time, Mandy dropped her handkerchief. The ticket taker bent to pick it up, and Kitty slipped past. Mandy was checked by the quarantine team. Her papers in order, she was let aboard. They hid between the large bales of cotton until the boat started moving swiftly up the river. Then Mandy stole two garment bags belonging to two women about their size. They switched the contents of the bags. Later when accused of stealing the bags, the contents were not those of the accuser. As they sailed away, Mandy knew that everything was now changed.

When the boat reached Greenville, Kitty dreaded what she had to do. Kitty gently took Mandy's hand. "This is where I get off. Thank you for getting me out of jail. But for your own good, you cannot be found with me. And our time is at an end. It is with deep sorrow that I leave you. The rest of your life is starting now. Girl, always put a smile on your face and don't take any wooden nickels."

Mandy felt like crying, but she knew Kitty would not tolerate that. "I will miss you. No matter how bad things got, all I had to do was yell for you, and you would make everything better. I will think of you always until we meet again. Stay safe."

The boat moved close to shore to take on coal. Kitty joined the refugees from yellow fever and jumped ship. Mandy stood on the deck, staring into the past for a long time. The boat started to move. Kitty was gone, and so was Mandy's childhood.

On Her Own and West

Mandy reached into her pocket. She now kind of wished she had not given Kitty the bulk of her money. She was hungry. So hungry she would have sold herself to get a steak. Barring that, she looked around the boat until she found a game, which she was able to enter. By the time the boat docked in Saint Louis, she was in better financial shape and had herself a good steak.

Saint Louis was controlled by the Union government, but many Confederate sympathizers also lived among the population in the city. Kitty's policy of no politics served Mandy well until one night when she was invited to a party. The party was held on Fifth Street, just south of Walnut. At first, things were going well at the party, and Mandy was enjoying herself. At about six o'clock, a large group of home guards came marching down the street. The people from the party started making fun of the marching "toy" soldiers. Mandy tried to discreetly step back into the shadows. The street filled with rowdy people. The spectators began shouting, hissing, and otherwise abusing the soldiers as they passed. Someone discharged a pistol into their ranks. The soldiers immediately turned and fired into the crowd. Screams and panic erupted. The whole column was instantly in confusion, breaking their ranks and indiscriminately discharging their muskets among people on the sidewalks. The shower of balls was terrible. Bullets were flying everywhere. No one was safe among the chaos. Mandy took refuge as best she could behind a large pillar.

The soldiers started going into buildings and arresting anyone who even looked like a Confederate sympathizer. Mandy was viciously pulled from her hiding place and quickly labeled as a rebel. She protested, telling them she was neutral. "In my business, it does not pay to take anyone's side of anything." But given her Southern way of speaking, her voice having more of a drawl than sweetness, the Union guard was not convinced. As a result, she spent the next two harrowing days in a dank, smelly jail cell. Then she was finally taken in front of the county court commission in a Baptist church.

The sneering captain of the guard felt Saint Louis could get along without the likes of her. He decided to banish her from the city. Mandy tentatively asked if she would be allowed return to her hotel room to gather her things. He replied that she could, but to make absolutely sure that she left town, he would personally escort her to the hotel.

The captain was not too bad looking—a little heavy and old but clean. Mandy was not surprised when they got to her apartment and he grabbed her, pulling her against his body. "You be nice to me and I might let you stay," he said with a greedy smile. "We can work something out. I am a busy man. I will only come to see you a few times a week. Of course, my men would like to visit occasionally too."

Mandy was surprised at how angry she got. Maybe it was because she was leaving town. Maybe it was just because she was sick of lascivious men. Or maybe it was because of her friends who had been shot in the street. Whatever the reason, she was angry and insulted. She grabbed a bottle from the small table in her room and quickly and efficiently hit him with it upside his head, knocking him out cold. He never saw it coming.

The captain's men in the hotel drawing room heard the ruckus. Instead of going to the captain's rescue, they celebrated what they thought was his conquest, knowing his intentions.

Meanwhile, Mandy took her garment bag and divested the captain of his wallet. She competently climbed out the window and did not stop running until she safely arrived at the stage station.

She bought a ticket on the first stage out. The stage was going to San Francisco, which suited her fine. She was finally going West as she and Kitty had dreamed about. Mandy thought that was about as far west as anyone could get. The station manager informed her it would be an hour's wait until the stage pulled out. "Can I sit in it?" Mandy asked, motioning to the empty stagecoach with wide-eyed excitement.

"This must be your first stagecoach ride. Sure, go ahead," he said indulgently. The driver, shotgun rider, and station manager kind of laughed. The driver got a stepping stool for her. "Welcome."

Mandy was enchanted and smiled from ear to ear. "Thank you, kind sir." The stage was egg shaped with leather curtains at the windows. It was bigger and roomier than Mandy thought it would be. She was glad to sit there in solitude and glad to be off the street in the event the captain woke up and came after her. Exhausted, Mandy soon fell asleep with a grin on her face. She later awoke when a man entered the stage.

"Hello. My name is Mr. Rogers. I did not mean to startle you." He was tall and well-dressed. His large body seemed to take up the whole stage. He sat down beside her. A woman followed him in and sat down across from her.

"Miss Jones. Pleased to meet you." Next came a gambler, a drummer, a cowboy named Paul, and three Union soldiers. Each tilted his hat and gave her a respectful greeting as they entered. This took Mandy by surprise as she was not used to politeness. But then neither was she dressed like a saloon gal.

Mandy thought it funny how the stage seemed very small now, with all the people crammed in it. They had to interlock their legs in the cramped space of the interior. The stage lurched forward as they started out. Mandy wanted to open a window to look out, but the others protested as they did not want the dust to come in.

"This must be your first trip on a stage," the cowboy said. "The only way to travel is in an alcoholic stupor," he said as he offered her a drink from his flask. She did want a drink but refused it because she wanted to stay clearheaded. As they traveled, the hours grew long, and the night was cold. Miss Jones organized an impromptu songfest. Mandy participated in this as it turned out to be all kinds of fun. At one point, the cowboy agilely climbed out the window of the moving stage and came back with a bedroll. Inside were blankets he shared with the group. He also offered them some jerky. Mandy did not know what jerky was, but she took it and ate it as she was hungry. It tasted salty but okay.

They rocked through the night, one bump after another. When morning broke, Mandy found she had rested her head on Mr. Jones' shoulder. She humbly apologized to him. He replied that she could rest her head on his shoulder anytime. Later, the men opened the stage window to shoot at wild animals, such as antelope and prairie dogs. This practice displeased Mandy who felt one should only shoot what one was going to eat. The passengers whiled away the long hours talking about Indian attacks and stagecoach holdups. The soldiers said they would protect the stage, causing the cowboy to laugh.

Mandy thought her bladder might burst. When the stage stopped, she took to the woods, thankful for the foliage cover. Upon returning to the stage, she found the stage driver had taken on a large load of mail that was shoved in among the crowded feet of the passengers.

The coach kept moving all through the day and night except for brief intervals at way stations. The stagecoach fare she paid did not include the cost of meals, at an average of a dollar three times a day. Mandy compensated by only eating one time a day. At other stops, she would walk around. She gave an excuse to the others that the stage rocking caused her stomach to be sick. This fooled no one as they saw her meticulously counting her money. A few times, one of the other passengers generously gave her rolls, saying they were given too much to eat.

Mandy was scared when the coach arrived at a river, but the coach was safely floated across. To the fourteen-year-old, it was all a great adventure. When they got to the way station at Molty Spring, the cowhand said he would not be traveling with them any farther. He offered to buy them all a farewell dinner.

Mandy was overjoyed by this announcement as she was beginning to be very hungry. The inn owner offered them some Tennessee whiskey. By this time, Mandy was really craving a drink. So she sat at the man's table, not knowing any better. The inn owner thought he would play sport of her and gave her a water glass full of white shine. All the men stared at her, mouths open, as she took her first sip. The drink was cool. The liquid rolled over her tongue like a refreshing waterfall. She kept it in her mouth to enjoy the fine brew. It burned a little as it warmed her stomach. She then took a drink. It was smooth and went down easier than Kitty's cheap morning whiskey. Mandy did not realize drinking by a lady in public was taboo. Drinking of white shine by a genteel woman was unheard of.

The cowhand laughed. "Good day to you. I hope our trails cross again. I think I would enjoy getting to know you."

Mandy smiled, realizing everyone now knew she was a lady of the evening. "Thank you for the meal and the drink."

The cowhand put his hat on. "Look out for those western coyotes."

Mandy smiled. "Never met a coyote I can't tame."

The cowhand winked. "Us western coyotes are a different breed than those New Orleans gents."

War between the States

Unknown to the driver, the Confederates, in preparation of a Union attack, burned the bridges north of Fort Wayne. When the stage came to the burned-out bridge, they were unable to proceed any farther. Anxious to be away from potential fighting and determined to get back on route, the stagecoach driver tuned and took an unknown route headed toward Missouri, hoping to reach the Democratic territory of Douglass. Then they turned west through the territory of Kansas. From the window of her stage, Mandy noticed they passed many militia units from both sides. She saw the rampant devastation that had been done to productive farmland. People in well-to-do clothes were now begging for food. Winter was upon them, and in some areas, soldiers were marching through the snow with no shoes on.

But the war had not really affected her until she heard that New Orleans was now occupied by Union forces. It was now under control by General Benjamin Butler, the "beast," and was under martial law. She feared for those she left behind, hoping they were safe.

Mandy had been dozing, but she was suddenly jarred awake when the stage jumped forward. It rocked violently. Then shots rang out. Mr. Rogers quickly grabbed her and pushed her down onto the rocking floor. Shots splintered through the cab of the stagecoach. Bullets whizzed past her head. Suddenly, she was covered with warm crimson blood. It seemed like water running through the strands of her hair. The heavy bodies of the unmoving men pinned her to the floor. The stagecoach came to a complete stop and lurched to the side. There were a few moments of silence. Then the door was wrenched open, and Mandy was viciously pulled from the coach by her ankles. The three Union soldiers who had traveled in the stage with her lay outside dead on the ground, their eyes staring and their uniforms coated in dark pools of blood.

One of the Confederate soldiers leaned over her, pulled her hair, jerking her head back, and spit in her face. "Hey, this one is still alive and pretty." Another Confederate soldier was pulling the other bodies from the stage, dumping them in a grotesque pile at Mandy's feet. Seeing the body of Miss Jones—her head half gone, eyes wide open, and a look of surprise etched onto her lifeless face—caused Mandy to close her eyes in horror. Mandy appeared to be the only surviving passenger. The mailbag was then pulled from under the seat of the stage and set on fire. The strong box was opened and the contents confiscated. Then the soldiers rounded up and took the horses from the stage.

"Let that one go! Can't you see she's a Southern belle?" a soldier on a very big black horse yelled. The men shrugged and moved off. The man on the big black horse rode close to her, threw her a sack of jerky, pointed, and said, "Go that way." He tilted his hat, turned the steed, and rode off without another glance.

Mandy just stood frozen in place for a long time. The night came quietly, eerie, cold, and pitch-black. Mandy still had not moved. She was in a state of shock. The quiet was unnerving. The trees seemed to grow fingers. Mandy moved close to the fire from the mail and sat until the fire burned itself out. There was no moon or stars in the sky. Everything was dark. Moving toward the stage, she tripped over the scattered bodies. She pushed herself back up in horror. Once she found where the stage was, she wearily crawled inside and hid in a curled-up ball for the remainder of the night. No sleep would come.

She was startled by the boom of cannon fire as daylight broke. Mandy cautiously found the courage to peek out the window. The grotesque bodies were still there. Gingerly stepping out of the coach, in abject fear she ran past the bloodied bodies to keep them from grabbing at her. After making her way down the road some distance, she stopped and fell to her knees. Taking a deep breath, she gathered herself and stood back up. She turned, determinedly went back, and searched the bodies in self-preservation. She got $4 from the drummer, two bits from each soldier, and $521 from the gambler. She took Miss Jones' bag as well as the garment bag she brought from the riverboat. After taking money from the dead, Mandy looked around to get her bearings and decide her next course of action. She had no idea where she was or where she should go. Looking at the stage, she decided to go in the direction the stage was pointed. She figured if she put one foot in front of the other, she would eventually end up somewhere. She was going to take to travel in the woods, thinking it was safer, but the sounds of war emanating around her stopped her. She continued down the rutted road. Her plan was to hide if she saw anyone at all on the road until she came to a town or a farm or something.

Walking all day, mostly uphill, she came to an overlook point. It was on a grassy knoll shaded by leafy trees. Down in the valley below were several hundred wagons and a multitude of Union soldiers. The site, although beautiful, sent chills down her spine. She was tired, cold, and hungry. It was getting late, and so she decided the overlook would be a good place to stay for a while. She found a secluded spot between two sheltering rocks and took a dress from the riverboat bag to use as a cover. Then she ate some jerky, settled down, and tried to sleep.

This night was light as it was enhanced by a full moon. Staring up at the twinkling stars, she wondered how the world could be so beautiful and yet so awful. Sleep was not to be had, as her mind was full of the horrors of war, death, and destruction. But she forced herself to be still and to rest as she listened to the noise from below. Mandy's eyes started to burn as the sun filled the sky with an array of reds, orange, and purple. At first, Mandy thought it looked wonderful. Then she realized something was burning. She sat up, looked down the mountainside, and saw there were no longer wagons or soldiers as had been there before. On the left, she saw many fires flickering. It looked like barns, houses, and wagons were all burning. The flames grew higher as more buildings and brush caught. The heat had to be intense as she could feel the fringes of it the whole way up on the mountainside where she hovered.

Black soot and hot embers rained down from the sky, turning everything dark. She moved to a spot under a rocky overhang to get away from the falling cinders. Every building in the city below seemed to be on fire. Moving farther to the left, she could see a bunch of Union soldiers dragging people from buildings and shooting them right out in the street. She could hear the horrible screams. Dense smoke arising from every direction marked the destruction of the city. The homes were ransacked. Women with children clinging to them ran helplessly down the road toward the river, desperately looking for escape. There was no aid nor protection afforded to the women, a fact that many drunken soldiers were taking advantage of. Mandy watched as a large group of women reached the river. Steamboats appeared to be packing everyone they could onto the boats.

Mandy turned and started running down the opposite side of the mountain. She did not know where she was going but knew she wanted no part of whatever was happening on the left side of the hill. Coming to a road, she moved swiftly away from the city, but not fast enough. She was surrounded and captured by a group of soldiers.

The soldiers dragged her hands behind her back while they searched her and found her large sum of money. They roughly pushed her ahead of them and took her to a building occupied by the higher-ranking soldiers.

The captain looked at her and the large sum of money, and he declared, "You have been collecting money for the rebellion. You are a spy."

Mandy could not admit to them she took the money from the bodies of the dead. She told them she got the money from playing poker. They did not believe her, sending her to the third floor of the building to await transport to a trial in St. Louis. The room was dark, damp, and reeked of the metallic odor of blood and rotting bodies.

The Confederates

There were other women and children also ensconced in the airless room. Forlornly sitting on the floor in the room, Mandy did not realize she was muttering aloud when she said she wished someone would tell her what was going on.

A little girl with disheveled blond hair and blue eyes, nine or ten years old, sitting next to her, peered up at her. In response to Mandy's words, she said, "Those damn Yankees killed my pa, grandpa, and my baby brother. They burned our crops and took Mom's hope chest that Pap made her. They set us walking. Then other red legs made us come here. All because they want us to pay them to make the laws instead of us making the laws." A tear seeped from her eye, leaving a trail as it snaked down her dirty cheek. "They killed my dog, and I do not know where they took my mother. If I get a chance, I will kill every Jayhawker in the whole world!"

In a lowered voice, Mandy tried to warn the child that she must be quiet and not let the guards hear her. Mandy felt very old and weary as she put her arm around the frail child and pulled her into her embrace to comfort her. She wanted to tell her that everything would be okay, that they would find her mother, but she knew better. "What's your name child?" she asked.

"Mary Gerson," she sobbed.

Mandy found an old bent nail lying in the debris on the floor. She picked it up and stabbed it into her own finger, drawing crimson blood. Then using her finger, she wrote on the wall behind her with her blood, "Mary Gerson was here, nine years old, looking for mother." When finished, she wiped her finger on the side of her dress and smiled down at the child. "There now, your mother will be able to find you."

The young girl knew in her heart Mandy was lying, but it made her feel better anyway.

Two huge burly men holding a bullwhip came up to the room full of prisoners. The prisoners cowered in terror. They walked between the women, looking them over, and stopped in front of the young girls. Pointing at Mary, the soldier commented, "That one is the daughter of Gerson, bushwhacker from way back."

One of the guards grabbed hold of the girl by her arm. Mandy immediately jumped up and kicked the guard hard on his shin. He dropped the little girl out of surprise. She quickly sprinted over to the other side of the small room and was surrounded by a group of women. The guard then grabbed Mandy, lifting her a few inches off the floor. "Hey, this is that good-looker spy. I will enjoy questioning her," he drawled with a leer. Mandy struggled and kicked out at him. "Lots of spirit. I will beat that out of her." He threw her down the staircase, bouncing her off the rough wall. He pushed her into a small room with no furniture.

For the next hour, Mandy was questioned about the sum of money they found on her person. She stuck to her story, knowing the truth would bring her even worse treatment. One guard started undressing Mandy with a look that had nothing to do with state rights. She hit him as hard as she could. He returned it in kind, the sound reverberating through the room. He then tied her by her hands to a wooden post. She was afraid of what was going to happen to her next, when one of the other guards yelled, "Let's get out. It's going to go!"

As the guards deserted her and ran, she realized she was tied to the only post in the basement. With a fierce rumble, the floors above her began to sag, cracks appeared in the walls and ceiling, and plaster rubble rained down on her. The falling plaster coated everything in a fine layer of chalky dust. With a roar, the building collapsed. Mandy watched in horror as bricks, plaster, wood, and bodies fell past her, landing in piles all around her. Only the front of the building was still standing as the cloud of white dust cleared. Mandy watched as surviving women struggled to unearth themselves. She then saw the front wall rocking, like a tree blowing in the wind. Women were busy pulling others from the rubble as the wall fell in. The vibrations and falling bricks caused the pole to which Mandy was tied to also topple. Stunned, she laid there in the rubble, staring into the eyes of a dead woman, unable to move or even look away. The world went dark as she passed out.

When she next awoke, she was lying on the hard ground outside, wrapped in a blanket. Several women wrapped in bandages lay on the ground next to her. The somber sound of children crying filled the air. There was something else—the smell of food. Struggling to sit up brought the attention of a Confederate soldier. "You're awake. We were worried you never would."

She put her hand to her pounding head. "Is there any food?" she asked in a weak voice.

The soldier smiled. "I am afraid we have only biscuits and soup." He disappeared and returned with the sparse food. The hard biscuits and the watery soup tasted wonderful to her. "Slowly," the soldier told her as he gave her the tin cup. "You're that spy from New Orleans." Mandy was more interested in the food than what the man was saying and did not respond. The soldier said, "Gerson wants to talk with you once you get something in your stomach."

She was taken to a khaki canvas tent that smelled of mold. Inside sat three men behind a makeshift desk. The tall one on the right spoke, "Come in. This is the spy from New Orleans. I have been told she saved my Mary from interrogation."

Mandy said, "Is Mary okay? I could not find her. Is she okay?"

Gerson replied, "She is alive but hurt badly. We need to know what contacts you have. Do you know of a safe house that can be used to house the homeless?"

Mandy replied, "I have no knowledge of any contacts. I am not a spy. I am neutral. In my profession, it does not pay to take anyone's side on anything!"

Gerson asked, "You do not support state's rights or home rule?"

Mandy replied, "I do not understand any of that stuff nor do I care to. I was forced to leave my home in New Orleans because of this insane war. Now I am just trying to make it to the West!"

Curious, Gerson asked, "What's in the West?"

Mandy replied, "There's money to be made in the West and no law dogs to take the profits."

One of the other men asked, "What is it that you do?"

Mandy haughtily replied, "I am an entertainer."

Gerson slyly asked, "Have you entertained the Union soldiers?"

Mandy, head held high in the air, said, "Soldiers cannot afford me."

Gerson stated, "Is that so?"

A very large strong man came up behind her. He said, "Who said we were going to pay?"

Mandy let the blanket slide off her shoulders, put her hand on her hip, and stuck her leg out. "You can rape me, but I will not move. I will just lie still. You will not enjoy it any more than the knothole in a tree, which I am sure you are used to." This brought laughter from the group.

The big man also laughed. "How can anyone be neutral in this war given the destruction inflicted on the South?"

Mandy covered her leg back up and stared the big man in the eyes. "War is an insanity only men can understand. You all are using what you call an honorable cause to justify unspeakable injustice inflicted on the innocent."

The big man said, "You are lucky you're a woman. God is on the side of the rightest."

Mandy said disdainfully, "Don't blame God for the sins of this insanity. The insanity exists for the enjoyment of men and for no other reason."

The bushwhackers were insulted. Although they were aware things might have been getting out of hand, they felt totally justified in their actions. The thought of executing her on the spot ran through their minds.

Gerson spoke, "I have been told you saved my daughter Mary from unspeakable horror. For that, I am grateful. You have your freedom to leave this camp now, but we have many needs. Many are sick or wounded. There are many refugees. A lot of them are orphans. There is a great need for nursing help and in help to prepare food for so many. Your help is greatly needed here. You have not pledged allegiance to the North yet have not pledged allegiance to the Southern cause. Therefore, although we would appreciate your help, I will thank you not to involve yourself with any of my men."

Because she had nowhere to go and no money and because she would at least have food and shelter at the camp, she decided to stay for a while and help where she could. Once she figured out where she could go and how to get there, she would leave.

The Camp

Mandy had never before taken care of children and was not good with them. These children had been severely traumatized. Their eyes were dark and hollow. They just wanted to sit and cry. They beseechingly asked for their parents—parents who would never return to love them. Mandy did not know how to handle their sadness or fears. She could not comfort them. She herself had been taught from a young age never to show emotion.

Therefore, when asked to help with the sick and wounded, she jumped at the chance but was surprised at the amount of wounded. Men, women, and children were lying shot and wounded on the cold ground. Without any medication to speak of, giving comfort for the pain was not easy. Mostly, her job was to keep them clean and fed, with very little food supplies.

After a while, she got the job of assisting the doctor. That meant taking amputated body parts out of camp and burying them. The camp's so-called hospital tent was hell on earth. The surgeon would stand over the operating table for hours without letup. Men screamed in delirium. Mandy would often be grabbed onto by a dying man who thought her a loved one. Many men eerily lay in total silence under the effect of shock.

Mandy was also in charge of picking up an instrument dropped by a doctor, washing it, then returning it to the surgeon. The worst of all were the men tagged as too far gone who were just left to die outside the tent. The cruel or heartless doctors did nothing for them. Mandy was their only comfort.

One day after digging many large shallow graves to accommodate the severed limbs, Mandy decided to get a jump on the next day's work. She dug an extra grave before heading back to the main camp.

On the way across the rugged ground, she fell. She was so exhausted the cold, hard ground felt so good she just lay there until peaceful, wonderful sleep fell upon her. She abruptly awoke to screams. Rousing herself and looking down the hill, she saw that some soldiers were attacking the camp. Amid all the chaos, she stayed hidden where she was. When the smoke finally cleared and the sounds dissipated, she would walk among the dead in silence, many of them innocent children she had cared for. When Gerson and his men returned, she was unable to relate what happened.

Gerson decided she was no longer of any use but still felt grateful to her for helping Mary. He had her taken to a nearby town and dropped off in the middle of the street with no money and only rags on her back. The local sheriff, not happy with her presence, took her to the jail. She explained to him she was neutral and wanted to go to the West to make some money. The sheriff took pity on her, but he still didn't want her in his town. The sheriff introduced her to a wagon master who was willing to let her join the train in return for her favors. He was not a bad-looking guy, and he would treat her well. She agreed as she felt she had no other choice and was glad to be on her way at last.

The Wagon Train

The wagon master was an older rugged man, trail dirty and with callused hands. He had contracted with Mandy for her passage on the wagon train. She was to ride with him and share his wagon for the duration of the trip. He was pleased with what he saw in Mandy, for she was young and attractive. Because her clothes were in tatters, he got her a plain, inexpensive, homespun beige dress to wear on the journey so she would blend in. In some ways, he was kind, but he demanded more from Mandy than she was willing to give. He liked it rough. Although not badly hurt, she found the bumpy, jarring wagon ride painful, so she chose to walk alongside.

Life on the trail was regimented. At four o'clock in the morning, a trumpet would sound, alerting everyone in the group that it was time to start the day. Mandy would fix breakfast of bacon, corn porridge, and johnnycakes. Then she would wash the pans and stow the bedding away. The walk would begin—fifteen miles until the next campsite. There she would unpack and make supper. Others would join into small groups to talk and sometimes to play music. The wagon master did not allow her to join in or to leave his wagon. She was not to mingle with the others. So after supper, she would obediently go wait in the wagon to pay for her passage.

The ladies from the train, surmising she was a victim of the war, helped her make a prairie dress. All the ladies wanted to feed her, as she was so skinny. They were under the impression she was the wagon master's wife, due to his possessiveness and her staying with him in his wagon. Mandy made no attempt to discourage this assumption, although she never lied about the arrangement. With time, the dark circles under her eyes disappeared. She regained some weight. The haunting deep look of shock left her eyes. As time went on, it was replaced with a sparkle of life and the excitement of the future.

The wagon master was the first to notice the improvements. One night, he was taking his due when he realized how really beautiful she was. The following day, he had trouble keeping his mind on his work. His mind kept straying back to Mandy. He rode ahead, stopped at a small town, and bought Mandy a dress. This time, it was not a plain serviceable dress. As he rode back to the train, he thought about her being from New Orleans. He was not sure why he was so smitten with her. It bothered him that he was. He thought maybe she might be a witch trying to take his soul. Perhaps he was under a spell. He could not find an explanation for his growing attraction to her.

He took her into a copse of trees and gave her the bundle he brought. Mandy thought they were going to have a picnic under the trees away from the train and was pleased. She was surprised when she opened the bundle and, instead of picnic fare, saw the dress.

It was a fancy dress. She gave him that saloon-gal smile she learned long ago, for she now knew why he brought her to this isolated place. She would have to pay for the dress.

The wagon master was surprised that Mandy was not shocked but committed the act without any argument or discussion. Mandy thought this would have cost him a lot more than a dress in New Orleans. The act completed, Mandy washed in a nearby stream, then put on the sparkly lace working girl's dress. It emphasized her figure and left her shoulders bare. The wagon master had been napping in the grass. He roused himself and looked up at Mandy drying her long red hair in the sun. The sequins on the dress reflected the sunlight, as ice would on a frozen lake. She was stunning. He now felt in his heart she was a voodoo woman and had put a spell on him.

When they returned to the train with Mandy clothed in her new sparkly dress, a rumble of whispers from the others met her. The ladies, once her friends, now pointed at her, whispering. Young boys snickered at her bare legs, causing their mothers to whisk them away. Mandy knew that look. She had seen it on the faces of the good ladies of New Orleans when they looked at Kitty. Now they knew what she really was. She knew it would not be long before she would be asked to leave the train. She hoped it would be near a town.

The wagon master came to her that very evening. He told her she was to be put off the wagon train in Lawrence, Kansas. He told her about the Eldridge Hotel in Lawrence. "You can get work there. Most of the men are Union, so be careful of your speech and be careful not to say anything about Gerson. Don't say anything about being at the rebel camp," he advised her.

True to his word, Mandy was put off the train the minute they arrived in Lawrence. She stood alone and watched as the wagon train rolled down the street of Lawrence, getting smaller as it went. She was sad to see this part of her life over but was ready to find out what the future held.

Lawrence, Kansas

Straightening her back with determination, Mandy turned and entered the Eldridge Hotel. It was an old but stately establishment, not as ornate as the gambling houses in New Orleans. She immediately pinpointed the man who ran the house by his dress and attitude and the way he sized her up. He sauntered over, looked her up and down, and inquired, "How old are you?"

Mandy shifted her weight, knowing it did not really matter. "That depends on the date," she answered.

The owner replied, "August 20, 1863."

Mandy smiled. "I must be fourteen, although I am not really sure. In my profession, we often have birthdays just to have the party."

The owner approached her, laying his hand on her bare shoulder, then letting it slip slowly and lingeringly down her body until it rested on her left hip. "You know, as the owner, I am rightly entitled to fifty percent, and I ride for free." Mandy was not happy with the terms but had little choice as she had neither food nor money. It was agreed.

After the owner, her next client was James Henry Kane, known to her as the butcher of Osceola. As she lay under him, she tried to keep her mind occupied elsewhere. She wondered how long it had been since she stood on that hill watching the plundering of Osceola. Once he was serviced and sleeping, she wrapped herself in a robe and stepped out on the back stairs of the hotel to get the predawn fresh air. A bakery was nearby, and the smell of freshly baked bread permeated the air. Instead of soothing her, what she happened to see in the morning light frightened her to the bone. Off to the east, she saw several heavily armed columns of riders approaching. She guessed there were about 460 men riding fast in her direction. Her hopes that this might be a peaceful interlude were dashed when the riders appeared. At the entrance to the town, numerous tents held a detachment of soldiers from the other side. They were overwhelmed by the numerous riders and fired upon. Immediately, men tried running for escape to the river, but they did not make it. They were ridden down and killed.

The riders then boldly rode down the main street shooting at everything they saw. Colonel Antrel, whom she recognized from the Confederate camp, fired his gun only twice before looking up at her and entering the hotel. James Kane, having been awakened, was now aware of the grave danger he was in. He grabbed his boots, jumped out a back window, and ran and hid in a cornfield, coward that he was. Mandy barely had time to pull on a dress before the riders swarmed the hotel. Mandy was accosted and dragged down the steps by some of the riders to stand in front of Antrel. He smiled. "Well, well, if it is not little Miss Neutral," he sneered.

Mandy stood straight and tall. Looking the bushwhacker in the face, she replied, "Well, well, if it is not the man with a just cause."

Antrel sneered, "You will entertain anyone."

Mandy replied, "I will sleep with the devil as long as he does not have any wooden nickels."

Antrel said, "Rightly so. You know I can justifiably shoot you as a Union spy."

Mandy challenged him, "Go ahead. If this is all life has to offer, oh well."

Antrel pulled a long sharp knife out of its scabbard, held it menacingly close to her throat, then cut through the straps of her dress. "Maybe I'll have all that glorious hair cut off and send you naked out into the streets."

Mandy gritted her teeth but stood firm. "Go ahead. It does not matter. But know in your heart you do this for no other reason than fun, for there is no just cause that would justify your actions today."

Antrel then grabbed her by the hair, dragged her out the door and through the street, and tied her to the city well. "It is too bad we have chosen not to wage war on women." Then he spit in the dirt at her feet, turned, and joined the other riders in their havoc.

Secured as she was near the prominent street, she could not avoid watching for four horrific hours as Antrel turned the town into a bloody and blazing inferno. People were savagely murdered. Structures were set afire. Violence ran rampant. It was all the more horrible knowing there was nothing she could do for the poor townspeople. As the ruffians finally rode out of town, Mandy sank to the ground at the side of the city well. Destruction was everywhere, and the fire was still burning brightly, too close to her. Although her hands were tied, she shaded her face from the extensive fire. Her hands burned and blistered, not from the flames but from the intensive heat. Flaming boards and burning hay bales were caught up in the high wind caused by the hot air meeting the cool of the night and swirled around her. It was calling to her like the Mississippi River used to so long ago, demanding her death to stop the destruction. Her eyes burned from the smoke. Her throat burned, making it so she could not scream.

When the sun finally peeked through the whole smoke-filled sky, fresh air blew down the bluff. Only then did Mandy know she was alive. Alive to bear witness. People passed by her with bodies carried on boards or in buckets. Their posture was one of utter defeat. Bedraggled women too shocked to cry walked in silence, carrying their beloved sons who were burned beyond recognition.

Mandy got the attention of a woman who had stopped to rest, for she was pulling a makeshift travois filled with many bodies. Coming over to Mandy, the desolate woman untied her and asked her for help before collapsing in a heap on the charred ground. Frightened but grateful to be free, Mandy drew water from the well. The bucket came up full of soot, but Mandy soaked a rag torn from her petticoat and wiped the old lady's soot-covered perspiring face. Mandy then tried to get some drinking water from the well, but the bucket got caught on something. Peering down the well, she saw the floating bodies of two unfortunate young men. Closing her eyes for a moment, she told the old woman that the well was dry.

The woman asked for help to get her men to the Old Oak Cemetery. "There are no coffins available, and the summer heat demands immediate burial. I do not want my young girls to see their father and brother like this. I cannot do it alone. Please help me."

Mandy's hands, being burned, made it impossible for her to pull the rope on the travois, so she tied the frayed end of the rope around her waist. The woman showed her the way to the graveyard, and they somberly trudged toward it.

At the gate of the cemetery stood an elderly woman taking names. The old woman spoke the names of her men. The lady at the gate said, "Eighty-nine, ninety, ninety-one, ninety-two, ninety-three. Put them in the row by the bluff."

Mandy forgot the pain in her hands as she tried to respectfully unload the bodies of the men. Thankfully, other women facing the same situation came to help. Mandy tried to show proper respect for the dead. This was hard to do, for the deceased were placed touching each other to make enough room for more bodies. When the larger men were unloaded from the cart, underneath there lay another body of a young man, maybe fifteen. Others had already placed more bodies in the mass grave. The old woman and Mandy desperately wanted the boy to be buried next to his kinfolk. Mandy tried to rearrange the bodies, but a fight with other bereaved women ensued.

A nearby Union officer intervened and broke up the fight. He was six feet and six inches, handsome, and with light-brown hair and blue eyes. "Haven't we had enough bloodshed for one day?" he asked as he picked Mandy off her feet and set her gently on the ground. The old lady started to cry, interspersed with soulful moans. Mandy explained the situation regarding the placement of the young boy's body. The gallant officer said he was taking charge and dispatched his men to the gate of the cemetery. "We will see to the burial." He took the old lady's arm and reassured her. "I will personally see that your son lies with his father," he said softly.

Mandy did not believe him, but the lady was appeased and seemed to calm down. He gave Mandy a shy half smile. "I hate to ask but could you use your travois to help others? We have a great need." She complied. Burial of the dead went on deep into the night. Mandy would make nine more rigorous trips up the cemetery hill. Lanterns lit the trail of the women who brought the dead from downtown to the hilltop graveyard.

Everyone struggled to make some sense out of the events of this day. When the sun came up, the task turned to digging through what was left of the city. Some were digging with hopes to find something to start over with. Some were solemnly digging for bones of the dead.

The sun found Mandy resting under a large maple tree. The town itself was still burning in places. Shivers ran up her spine as she tried to logically figure out what to do next. She was coated with soot and had several burns. She was dizzy, nauseous, and extremely exhausted; and she hurt all over. Looking down the hill, she watched as the young Union officer and his small regiment set up an aid station and a tent to treat the eight. Supplies were pouring in from sympathetic surrounding counties. A long line of gray wagons moved slowly through thick black mud. The horses were covered with sticky soot. They seemed to have trouble breathing in the hot smoke-filled air. Many wagons were forced to pull over to the side.

Mandy gazed down at her hands which were blistered from the burns. They were red and painful. Seeing a horse trough, she sought relief from the water within it. The water was black with soot, but the cool water relieved the pain somewhat when she dipped her hands in it. She rested her head against the side of the wooden trough, closing her eyes and praying that yesterday was just a dream. She was afraid to open her eyes to find it was real.

Her moment of peace was disturbed by an older Union doctor. "Get your hands out of that!" he yelled.

Looking up, she saw all the destruction and yelled back, "Mind your own. Leave me alone!"

The doctor yelled, "That water is contaminated! Those burns will get infected. I don't want to have to remove your hands. I do not have time to waste on stupidity."

That young handsome Union officer strode over and slowly pulled her hands from the water. She turned and sought comfort from his huge, strong chest. The doctor went into action and applied sulfur to her burns. As he did so, severe pain ripped through her. The doctor was busy wrapping her hands when a woman ran up yelling.

"Come quick, Doctor. My son was shot. He was under the hay. I just found him. Please come quick!"

The doctor quickly finished the bandaging. He closed his eyes for just a second, then stood. "You keep your hands clean. If you had taken care of them in the first place, they would have been showing signs of healing by now. Get her something to eat and find a place for her out of the sun." He then ran off to follow the lady who needed help.

"Excuse Doc. He has had a hard night. I am James Jefferson Russell. Please come with me. I saw you at the cemetery yesterday. You were great," the Union officer said as he offered his arm and helped her to her feet.

She smiled back at him. "I am Amanda Arness, very pleased to meet you. Please do not take me to the aid tent," she said with a pleading look on her face.

The young Union officer wondered how she knew about aid tents. He did not ask about it but instead just found her a seat in the shade of a large sheltering tree and got her some grub to eat. "Do I know you?" he turned to her and asked.

Mandy looked closely. "I don't know. I am from New Orleans. Have you ever been there?"

"When I worked for the K ranch, I would make supply runs through New Orleans. I did not like it much. I spent most of my time down by the river. Well, I better catch up with Doc." He tipped his hat, then was gone.

When Mr. Russell and Doc returned, they were surprised to hear sweet singing coming from the aid tent. Pulling up the flap, they were astonished to find Mandy dancing and singing as she moved between the beds.

She abruptly stopped when she saw the doctor. Slipping past them, she said, "Yesterday was a day to cry. Today is a day to sing, for we are still alive." Then she slipped out of the aid tent and was gone.

The Union officer set up passage available for anyone who wanted to leave the city. With no money and knowing no one in the city, Mandy decided it was a good idea and a good time to get out.

The Mining Town

Mandy knew she would not get very far without any money, so when some men decided to go to a mining camp, she went with them. They were a jovial group, easy to get along with. Once there, Mandy was welcomed to the mining town. She found herself set up in a small but nice cabin. It had a door with a wooden latch, a fireplace made of sod, and a bunk. She even had a window. It was small but brought in some light, and it enabled her to look out on the countryside. The cabin had two shelves and a bench, all made with a nice slab of rock. She had a row of nails to hang up her things. She got herself a bucket for water, a writing table, and an oil lamp. Mandy even got herself a book. Once a week, the book could be traded in for a different one. Her schooling stopped when her mother died, so her reading was not so good. But with the help of some of the men, she learned. All in all, it was humble, clean, and nice. She was content.

When the harsh winter arrived, the cabin was very dark and dreary. But it kept her sufficiently warm throughout the winter season as it was well-built. Then spring came, bringing rain, and the cabin was very wet and damp. In fact, the rain indoors continued three days through the roof after it quit outside. Finally, summer came, bringing unbearable sweltering heat. Seasons changed.

The camp had no official laws. Gambling, brawling, telling yarns, drinking whiskey, and buying Mandy's time filled the men's leisure hours. Sundays broke the boredom, for it was not a workday. Even though there was no church building, Mandy was expected to attend a meeting every Sunday. Not to do so would have been thought of as neglecting her religion and an insult to the town. So on Sundays, they would all assemble and sit on cured buffalo hides spread on the ground. The only women in attendance were a few squaws and

Mandy. She learned that a person had to be mindful as to his mouth, for isolation and built-up energy led to frequent fights among the burly men. These meetings would often end up in a free-for-all fight.

The mining town did not get regular deliveries of goods. By the time springtime arrived, supplies had become scarce. One day, several wagons heavily loaded down with supplies showed up. It was a time to celebrate with fresh coffee, candles, and, best of all, a group dinner. The miners, for the most part, spent their lives alone in solitude digging their claim. After a long cold winter, a fresh hot meal was like heaven to them. After the group dinner, there was singing and dancing. Each man happily took a turn swinging Mandy around. By the end of the day, she was very tired but in a good, satisfied way. Most of the men brought her a gift as a thank-you for keeping them company during the long, cold winter months.

One day, a lucky miner struck a big vein of silver. Word of a silver strike quickly spread throughout the land. The news of the strike brought in people, merchants, and industry to the small town, hoping for prosperity. A general store was built, and a blacksmith shop sprung up. The town and population grew. Big houses with fancy women went up almost overnight. Mandy, being the "old" girl in town, found herself sitting alone in her small humble cabin. She had two choices—go to work in one of the big houses or leave town altogether. A sporting house situated in a mining town was set up for the purpose of getting money and for no other reason. Mandy had heard stories of women being beaten if they could not get a man to talk with them and beaten if he did not buy a drink and, worst of all, she had absolutely no right to refuse a man anything. It was a dismal prospect and not for her.

Giving up the small cabin that she called home was a difficult choice for Mandy. She had grown accustomed to the small town and the miners. She enjoyed having her own home. But she decided to get out while the getting was good. So she packed her bag with her meager belongings and caught a ride on a supply wagon headed east. *Oh well*, she thought. It might be a long time before someone going West would take her with them. With sadness, she bade goodbye to the small mining town that had been her home.

Dodge City

The wagon's first stop was Dodge City, a populated but dirty cow town that relied on the revenue from the herds being driven through. When she arrived, it had been raining for three days straight and the streets had turned to a disgusting river of mud. Mandy was soaked to the bone when she jumped off the wagon in the dreary weather. She sank in the muck up to the top of her buckle-up shoes. Thankfully, she had the good sense to hold her dress high above her knees. She spotted a diner and trudged her way over to it. It had real table-cloths and napkins. The food tasted great, the coffee even better. The Rathbone stove just inside the door provided warmth against the damp chill, a warmth she had not felt since she started on her long and arduous journey.

She was tired, wet, hungry, and sloshing around in wet, muddy shoes. Social norms be darned, she removed her soaked shoes and placed them under the stove to dry. Her actions caught the attention of the respectable ladies of the town, who started whispering with such a force the owner was alerted to the situation. The restaurant owner, in turn, requested the help of the local marshal, who happened to be there at the diner having his lunch.

The marshal resignedly pushed his lunch aside and approached Mandy. She looked up to see a very tall handsome man with a huge hat standing before her. He stood about six feet and six inches with light-brown hair and blue eyes. Very blue eyes. Sounding a little embarrassed and very shy, he asked, "Pardon me, ma'am. Are you new in town?"

Mandy knew exactly what the problem was but was too tired, too wet, and too cold to be pushed, even by this giant of a man. So she smiled that learned smile. "Yes, sir. I got in this morning.

Won't you please join me?" She tipped her head and nodded at the adjacent chair.

The huge handsome marshal pulled out the chair and sat down. "I am sure, you not being from the city, that you are uninformed as to our custom of not removing our shoes in a public place."

Mandy then smiled a genuine smile. "My feet are so very wet and cold. I did not mean to offend anyone. I just wanted to partake of some food and get warmed up."

The marshal now had a problem. She admitted she knew it was wrong to put her shoes under the stove but made no attempt to rectify the situation. "I guess now that you have had a chance to get warm, you will be putting them back on," he said with an understanding smile.

She looked at the shoes. They were caked with mud and had red water pooling around them. She knew how uncomfortable it would feel to put them back on her feet. She sighed. "I am enjoying this delicious coffee that I have paid for. The wagon I rolled in on will be leaving soon. I hope to be dry and fed when I get back on that wagon, for it may not stop in another town for several days. I am sure your town will not be damaged too much by my presence for that small amount of time."

The marshal realized that politely asking this woman for anything would do no good. He would have to get forceful to make her remove her soddened shoes from under the stove and cover her bare feet. Although it was extremely poor manners, she hadn't broken any law. He thought it best to just enjoy his coffee and let her leave town quietly, to the disgust of the good ladies of the town. Smiling at her, he looked directly into her eyes and asked, "How are your hands?" She looked down at her hands, then up at him in confusion. He then said, "Lawrence, Kansas. I remember it like it was yesterday."

Mandy broke into a smile. She thought he looked familiar. "I try not to remember it at all. I keep hoping it was all just a bad dream."

Some ruffians entered the restaurant, spied Mandy at the table drinking her coffee, and approached her. "We are about to move the wagons out, but we've got bad news. Instead of continuing on, we are headed back to the mining camp. They sent the local store owner a substantial new order. We've sold everything we had. Are you coming back along with us?"

Mandy reached over to get her shoes from under the stove. She made her decision quickly. "No, I reckon I'm not. But thank you kindly for bringing me this far."

James smiled while he watched her face as she gingerly pulled on her soaked shoes. Meanwhile, the good ladies whispered louder. She pulled up her dress in order to lace up her shoes, and dirty water squeezed out with every hook. James's eyes moved from her face to those amazing long, soft, shapely, delicious, perfect legs.

She smoothed down her dress, coyly looked up at him, and said, "Are you going to run me out of town?"

James replied, "No, ma'am, you have committed no crime." He stepped out onto the street and watched her as she left. She kind of swayed as she made her way down Front Street. He watched her look over at the Dodge House and at the Long Tree before disappearing down a side street.

The good ladies thanked him for ridding them of such a wicked woman. "This town doesn't need her kind," they stated.

The marshal tipped his hat and thought, *That is exactly what Dodge needs.*

Later that night, James saw the captivating girl sitting at the Trail's End. He ambled over and addressed her. "Good evening. How are things going?"

Mandy looked up at him and smiled. "Buy me a drink, cowboy?" James searched his pockets and found two bits. They drank and talked for some time.

They seemed to have a comfortable connection with each other. Mandy, looking into his intense eye, felt she could trust him. Finally, James got up and stated he needed to do rounds and check on the town.

Some ruffians at the bar had been looking her way. They handed the bartender some money. Mandy closed her eyes and looked away. Her stomach turned at the thought of entertaining these ruffians. James, who hadn't yet left, understood the silent looks and felt the fangs of jealousy. He turned back to Mandy and asked, "Do you have your prostitution license?"

Mandy, at first, was surprised. She had heard of a prostitution license but never had one. She had heard they cost $10 and a trip to the doctor. She didn't have money for either of those things. The ruffians were staring at her when the marshal spoke. "I will fine both you and the man you are with if you practice the trade without a license." One of the ruffians came over to ask how much the fine was. The marshal, who had never fined anyone before, said off the top of his head, "One hundred dollars for her and seventy-five dollars for anyone I find with her." Mandy now realized what the tall handsome marshal was trying to do. The ruffians looked her over again, decided it was not worth it, then chose another girl.

After the marshal left, the owner of the Trail's End came out and told Mandy she could not work there until she got a license. Mandy was actually kind of happy she had been fired, as those men frightened her a little.

Her happiness was short-lived when she realized she had no place else to go. Once again, she stood on the sidewalk with no money and no roof over her head. She saw the big marshal come up the street. "Can I help you?" he asked, tipping his hat.

"No, thank you," she said sweetly. "I think you did enough."

James kicked at the dirt. "You don't want to work for those guys anyway. I have to come down two or three times a week because one of their girls got her face punched in. It is not a safe place."

Mandy tilted her head. "The job has its fallbacks. So do you know where I could get a room for the night?"

He took a protective stance. "I will take you to the boarding house on Front Street. The rates are low, and the rooms are clean." Just then, gunfire broke the silence of the night. James went into action, pulled his gun, and went out into the night.

After the marshal left, a tall, good-looking, well-dressed—for this cow town—man approached her. He was polite and talked for a while before asking her price. She told him she needed lodging for the night if he only wanted standard entertainment and was willing to pay for a room. The price would be $1. He felt the price of a room and a dollar was kind of high. Mandy confidently responded, "If you want the best, you pay for it." It was agreed. The man called himself John. Mandy knew that was a lie, but any name would do. It did not matter.

Once they got to the room, "John" demanded more than the standard roll in the hay. He claimed he could get five girls for the price of the room and a dollar. He wanted more and took a donkey punch. He had his way with her. The pain that shot through her body the night before was not eased by the morning light. She lay still, hoping the man would just leave. When he did, she struggled to get up and made her way to the water room at the end of the hall in order to get cleaned up. Returning to the room, she found the man was back, waiting for her. She informed him he had already gotten his due and that she was leaving. But he grabbed her with a viselike grip and threw her viciously down on the bed. Turning her over, he began pumping her from behind. When she began to think he would be finished, he yelled, "Ride 'em, cowboy!" and two other men came in the room and joined them. The long night turned into a long day. The men finally left her bleeding and bruised on the floor of the room.

As she lay in pain on the hard wooden floor, there was a knock on the door. A voice called out, "Check out time was ten o'clock. You will have to pay for another day." What a dilemma. The men were gone, and she had no money. Sore as she was, she awkwardly dressed and climbed out the window. Fearing the hotel clerk would be after her, she looked for a place she could hide. Spotting a staircase, she ran to the top and stood tight against the door, hoping she would not be spotted.

Hurt and Starting Over

As Mandy pressed against the door so as not to be seen, she heard a voice from behind the door yell, "Hold on. I am coming. I will be with you in a minute." She hurriedly pulled away from the door and started back down the steps, when the door was opened by Doc Stone. He looked at her, assessing the situation. She tried to talk her way out of entering the doctor's office, but he could see she had a need to see him. He also realized she was probably reluctant because she had no money with which to pay him. He was able to usher her in and allay her concerns. While treating her, he gently talked to her. She found herself talking back. In the course of the evening, they formed a friendship that would last the rest of his days.

Dr. Stone tried to talk her into going to the law to file a complaint, but Mandy knew the law was not meant for people like her. She would only accomplish being labeled as a troublemaker. She would possibly be tarred and feathered and ridden out of town. That is, if she was lucky. Doc had to admit that despite the valiant efforts of the new young marshal, Dodge City was still a wide-open town. He said, "Change is coming, but change takes time."

Doc Stone insisted Mandy stay in his cabin, a storage shack, until she got on her feet. It was not much, but at least it was warm and dry. She reluctantly agreed. Mandy was able to take some time to view the town of Dodge City while living at Doc's. She learned that north of town, the only activity was wagons stopping over on their journey West. That part of town would swell to over a thousand men, women, and children when the wagon trains came in. Then just as quickly, the population would drop to almost zero as the wagons, fully loaded with town goods, moved out. Nearby Fort Dodge was built to protect the settlers and the wagons from the Kiowa and

Cheyenne Indians. The fort also served as a supply base. Fort Dodge was also a main distributor of the US mail.

Dodge City was mainly a trading post, with whiskey and women being the most traded goods. Mandy learned it was wise not to be downwind of the stockyards and, even worse, the buffalo fields that were filled with thousands of uncured hides. Even after leaving that area, the odor permeated and stayed embedded in one's clothing.

The south side of town was a shanty town the end of the trail for those who lived there. It was full of impoverished, starving people who had nowhere else to go. They had no foreseeable future ahead of them. This was also a good place from which to stay away. Without any law to speak of, any dire thing could happen there.

On the hill overlooking Dodge City was Boot Hill, named because the men buried there died with their boots on. On the other hill were large houses, not as big as the plantation homes of the South but were showplaces of the rich. She certainly did not fit in there and never would.

Mandy decided the best place for her was on Front Street. The saloons were clean, and the cowboys were, for the most part, kept under control—as far as a woman would go, that is. That's not to imply it was not rough. Men got themselves shot every day for every sort of stupid thing. Mandy applied for work in most of the saloons on Front Street, but word of the marshal's interest in her had already spread throughout the town. No one would hire her without the required prostitution license. Mandy knew that most of the girls in Dodge City did not have one, but it was hard to fight city hall. She had imposed on Doc long enough.

It was raining the day Mandy made her way through the muddy streets to the city jail to get the license. Looking through the barred window of the small red brick building, she spied the tall handsome marshal inside. The marshal's sidekick was a thin handsome man who did not dress well and who had a limp as a result of the war. He was occupied making coffee.

Mandy wondered why she hated the thought of going in to apply for the license. She was not ashamed of her profession. A girl must do what a girl must. Taking a deep breath, she knocked on the wooden door.

"Come in. It's open," a friendly voice called from inside. Mandy's stomach turned as she stepped in. "Morning, miss. Please have a seat. Would you like some coffee? Brewed it today," Harford, the sidekick, said with a welcoming smile. The marshal seemed uninterested, sitting behind his desk, playing with some wanted posters. As Mandy sat down, Harford held her chair. "What can we do for you?"

Mandy always carried herself with confidence but now found herself without words. It was then that she realized she was attracted to that pain-in-the-neck marshal. She had been ever since the first time she met him down by the river. Stunned with this new knowledge, she could not make herself ask for a prostitution license. "I am new in town. I thought I could get someone to show me around," she said, kicking herself for not asking for the license.

"Why sure. It would be a pleasure."

At this, the marshal looked up from his work and said, "We are not running an escort service. Harford, I wanted you to go out and check on the Johnsons. They reported they have been missing a lot of chickens of late."

Harford started to stutter a response, as this was the first he heard about any missing chickens. Mandy stood up with dignity. "Well, if it is too much bother, I will find someone else," she said and stormed out.

Puzzled, Harford looked at James. "What the heck?"

James smiled. "I know what she really wanted. She needs a prostitution license."

Harford looked confused. "Aren't you going to give her one?"

James threw a pad on his desk. "I got it right here." He patted his pocket. "I don't know why I did not give it to her."

Harford smiled. *I do*, he thought.

Working in the Saloon

Meanwhile, Mandy was angrily stomping down the street as she was making her way back empty-handed to Doc's place. There was no way she was going to ask that overbearing mutton shunter for anything. In her distraction, she almost tripped over a man who came flying out of the Long Tree to land in front of her.

A big burly man followed him out, and the first man's hat was flung onto the dusty street. "Don't come back!" The bartender looked over at Mandy. After a brief consideration, he said, "You are a good-looking woman. Are you looking for a job?"

Mandy explained about lacking the license but said she could still sell drinks and deal.

The bartender shrugged and said, "What the marshal doesn't know won't hurt us. When the marshal is in town, you only deal and sell drinks. When he is out of town, you can use the room upstairs." They had a deal.

This worked out well. Mandy actually kind of liked the arrangement. The fact that she was new in town gave her reason to charge a high price. The owner of the Long Tree noted how well Mandy handled the men—from buffalo hunters, cowboys, outlaws, and farm boys. He heard stories about Mandy being a top New Orleans toffer from a brawl house. He decided to investigate. He hired Mandy for himself. He requested all kinds of things using slang that polite women would not understand. But Mandy, being an experienced naughty lady, just nodded understandingly and took his hand. He put her through the paces. Satisfied she knew what she was doing, he offered her a job as head lady, explaining most of the women who were hired by the Long Tree were fresh off the farm. They were okay for the first night but kind of ordinary and a little shy and unknowledgeable on how to please a man. "Dodge is known for 'Wham! Bam! Thank you, ma'am.'" He wanted a better reputation for his saloon. He wanted the Long Tree to be a first-class brothel with top talented girls, who were able to competently do anything a man asked for.

He gave her total control of the girls, with a high wage and a percentage of every cent the girls made. Mandy readily took the job, determined to make the Long Tree the best house in town.

She called all the girls downstairs for a meeting. It was midday and the women had not yet bothered to make themselves presentable. Mandy found this unacceptable. The first rule of the house would be that no girl left her room without being appropriately and enticingly dressed from head to toe. Mandy encouraged the girls to pick up whatever skills they could from their customers. Thus, they became very good conversationalists as a group, and many customers actually ended up as a regular patron of the girl whose interest and skills most reflected their own, rather than those whose physical attributes initially most appealed to them.

Mandy explained the basics to the girls. "Of course, nobody will be forced to have sex with anybody. You will have instances when you will have to decline a cowboy. You can walk out if a client repeatedly doesn't follow the rules. You must learn to fake enthusiasm for a guy if you are not immediately attracted to the guy. I try to find some common ground or something about him I like. I believe that a connection is important, especially if they're paying extra money for your time. Please know it is okay to enjoy sex. As you'll probably be working for a third of your life, it seems a real waste of your life to spend it hating what you do. This is a business. Treat it as such. Rich and successful men will take many women. Don't confuse business with any kind of commitment. As you get older, you will want to find different work. It is not nice to say but there are no old girls working at the Long Tree. If you want a relationship with a man, look for other work. There are no married women working at the Long Tree."

"If you respect your client, your client will respect you. If you treat your client as an animal, he will behave as one. There's no point in doing fifty men a week. It will only make you overtired and depressed. You will want to quit, and you will ultimately end up broke and unemployed. Ten men a week is a good amount. Of course, this number will go up when the herds move in. This cannot be helped. During that time, you all will be required to work a full shift. Know you will get extra time off when the herds move out. Anyone wishing to stay on when the herds move out will be called upon to help clean the Long Tree from head to toe. You will be paid to do this, but at a lesser rate. I will support you and look out for your welfare."

"Be prepared to encounter men who have a thousand excuses as to why they don't want to use condoms. Remind them that if you decide to make an exception for them, you've probably made exceptions before and you'd be putting them at risk. Remind them of their wives at home. Be firm and willing to walk out the door if they won't comply."

One of the girls asked who was going to pay for the required condoms as they cost about a week's pay.

Mandy said, "The Long Tree. By the way, if you get the clap, you will be fired. The Long Tree wants the reputation of being a clean place. Everyone will get a checkup with Doc every two months. Your employment is dependent on this."

Cookie spoke up, "You're making a lot of rules. We can get work just by walking out the door."

Mandy shifted her weight and put her hand on her hip. "The door is always open. I intend on making the Long Tree the highest-paying, most respected place in town. It will be the first place men stop at when they hit this town, but if you want to work in a dump with no protection, go ahead. If you want to work someplace else in the off season, okay as long as it is not in Dodge and Doc clears you for work when you return.

"The Long Tree will offer cowgirl, the pillow missionary, swimmer, sixty-nine, round the world, etc., on the regular menu. Your rate will be prorated to the task. Anything not on the menu must be cleared by me. Careful screening is the most important thing I will do for you. It is a protection from violence. I will keep you informed about known problem clients. Any man on the blacklist, you do not take, or you will be asked to leave. You are also required to report bad clients when asked."

Her training and work requirements were taken to heart by the girls at the Long Tree.

Soon, the sought-after girls would be referred to as Mandy's girls. It was not long until reputation and word spread throughout the town. That red-haired, sapphire-blue eyes, five-foot-eleven, 135-pound girl was the boss of the best house of pleasure in Dodge. Mandy herself took no clients but teased clients a lot. Word had it that Mandy was teaching her girls to satisfy in ways the cowboys had not even thought of.

James

As the Long Tree's reputation spread, the tall handsome marshal felt it his duty to check the situation out as he knew for a fact Miss Mandy had never gotten a prostitution license. He did not want any unsuspecting hardworking cowboy to get rolled or cheated in his town. He stood looking over the batwing doors of the Long Tree. The bar was furnished the same as it had always been but looked different somehow. The oak bar seemed to gleam with the reflection of the newly polished chandelier. The stained green felt that covered the tables now was replaced with new clean felt. The ladies moving about the room wore dresses that seemed to blend in with the table but were offset with bright-red sequins. The joint no longer smelled of vomit and cow dung but had a sweet smell of aged whiskey, good cigars, and creosote oil.

He spotted her over in the corner. Mandy looked dazzling in a sensational forest green knee-length dress with dainty lace and embroidery. Her hair had a distinct style, with tresses of ringlets and swirls with a long braided tail which folded around her head and was secured into a bun shape, decorated with light-green ribbons. It gave her a neat and graceful look. What captivated him the most were her eyes. That really set off the look. They sparkled of fire yet were filled with understanding and a hint of naughty impending sex. James stepped into the saloon and was surprised to find the floor was not sticky.

Mandy floated over to ask him if he would like a drink. Gazing upon her, he found his mouth dry. Suddenly, he was aware of how fascinatingly beautiful she was. Whatever he came to ask her was forgotten as she brought him a drink and waited for him to ask her to sit. This he did not do, but he just sat looking at her with the eyes of a grade-school boy on his first romp.

She placed two drinks on the table in front of him but still patiently stood. "Are you going to pay for those drinks?" The marshal did not pay for drinks in Dodge or anywhere else. He searched his pockets as she asked, "Would you like anything else?" After some hesitation, he asked her to sit.

"Don't do me any favors" was her droll reply.

Then from outside, someone shouted in and invited the marshal to a gunfight.

Mandy then felt a sense of panic. She had a very bad feeling about this. "Don't go, Jim!" she yelled imploringly as she grabbed his arm. "It makes no sense."

The man from outside yelled again. "I am calling you out, marshal! What's the matter? You chicken?"

"Stay inside," Jim grimly ordered as, without hesitation, he got up, went to the batwing doors, and stepped out into the sunlight. Mandy followed to the door, staying in the shadows.

The heckler was standing at the ready in the street, his hand over the gun in his holster. There was a cocky look on his face. There was twenty feet between them when they stopped to make their play. The marshal never cleared leather when the stranger fired his gun. The swiftness of the stranger was a shock to everyone. Mandy screamed as the marshal clasped his chest with a gasp and fell to the ground. A second bullet retort sounded as blood squirted out of James's head. Mandy ran to his side and knelt to pick James's bleeding head out of the mud.

Jim felt the burning bullet rip through his side and felt the blood running down his face and into his eyes. He felt the ground come up and hit him. He then felt her soft hands lifting him out of the dirt. Looking up, her beautiful soft eyes were filled with salty tears. He wanted to reach out to her to stop her from crying, to comfort her. The pain that the bullets caused was nothing compared to the pain in his heart caused by those tears. Suddenly, Doc was by his side, but the marshal could not comprehend what he was saying. He felt men picking him up and felt her hands slip from him. "No," he moaned, "let me die in her arms."

*****

When James regained consciousness four days later, it was her relieved eyes he saw first. No more tears, just smiles as she jumped up and got Doc. Mandy left the room shortly after he awoke, saying she had neglected her work of late, and since it was Saturday, she would be needed.

Several town women muttered as Mandy passed by and made her way to the Long Tree. The comment Mandy liked best was "What's that Jessabelle doing on the street while the sun is out? Why is it getting so decent people cannot walk the street?"

Mandy thought, *Yeah, you sure do soil the street.* But she smiled and said, "Good day, ladies. The sunshine is nice today."

The day did not get any better. It got much worse. When she entered the Long Tree, sitting smugly at the table known as her table, was the evil man who shot James. He mockingly held up a bottle and asked, "How's the marshal?"

"He'll live, no thanks to you. What are you doing still in town? You don't think you can shoot a United States marshal and stay in this town?"

Dan used his foot to push out a chair. He gestured. "Sit. I cannot leave town until the marshal is well and truly dead. I never leave a man half dead. He would then be compelled to come after me. I would spend all my time looking over my shoulder. It is better if we end it here. Sit. I already made a deal with the bartender for your time."

Mandy looked over at Joe, the bartender. He was sporting a black eye. His face was mottled black and blue, and his hand was wrapped up. "Is that so?" she drawled.

Dan said, "I always take the best. Sit. Or are you ready to go upstairs? You see, the way I figure it, that marshal ain't going to want to tangle with me no more, now that he knows how good I am. If'n he knows I have you upstairs, I won't have to go to the trouble to call him out again. He will come to get me."

Mandy laughed derisively. "I am nothing special to the marshal. He enjoys himself with many of the girls in town."

Dan briefly thought about that and said, "I am sure he does, but you're his girl. Why else would you have spent the last week hovering at his side?"

Mandy sat. "I often help Doc. Because I like the marshal does not mean the marshal likes me, any more than any of the other girls."

Dan smiled, showing his rotten teeth. "True enough, but I am going to spend my time with you anyway. Have to do something while he gets better."

Mandy raised an eyebrow. "Why not just go over to Doc's office and finish him off?"

Dan stood up and held her chair. "That would not be sporting of me. I want him well when I finish him off. Are you going upstairs, or do you want me right here? This table looks strong enough."

All eyes were on her as she stood and walked up those long steep stairs, head held high. He pushed her down the narrow hall and into her room. What followed in Mandy's room was constant misery as the man she hated moved his hated fingers all over her flesh. He seemed to have multiple hands reaching her, grabbing her. She heard him laughing, heard his taunting, degrading voice, as a violent devastating pain ripped her in half. He did everything he could think of to degrade her. Before falling asleep, he tied her facedown. She felt like a piece of trash, facedown, covered in his urine and palm prints. That sticky substance was all over her face. Even in the Kansas heat, she felt very cold. She forced herself not to cry as his weight pinned her down so she could not move, rendering her totally helpless.

Dan felt very robust and mighty having control of the marshal's woman, the toughest woman in Dodge. He enjoyed degrading her. That marshal may use other girls, but this one, this act would bring the marshal to a gunfight while distracted.

Meanwhile, Jim was recovering in Doc's office. He wondered why Mandy had not been up to see him since he woke up. Then again, he had given her no reason to think she was anything special to him. He remembered how he treated her the last time he was at the

Long Tree. He did not even invite her to sit. The funny thing was, he had always stood and let any other woman have his chair. What was it about this woman that made him act so badly? He finally admitted to himself it was fear. He was more afraid of her eyes than he was of a man with a loaded forty-five down in the street.

Doc thought James was asleep when Harford came to see him.

"I tell you, Doc, I got to do something. He has her up in that room like a prisoner doing God knows what to her. I can't just stand around."

Doc put his hand on Harford's shoulder. "Getting yourself killed will help no one."

Harford shook Doc off. "Maybe I can sneak up to her window and catch him by surprise."

Doc shook his head. "There's no way you can get up to the second story of the Long Tree with that bad foot of yours."

Jim had heard enough. He now understood why Mandy had not come to see him. Dan Clocker was keeping her against her will.

It had been three days since Dan took Mandy upstairs. Mandy walked slowly down the staircase in front of Dan into the full bar. Everyone stopped what they were doing and turned to stare at her. Dan pushed her to move faster. When she got to the bottom step, he hit her hard on the backside. "Grab a chair."

Men jumped to give her a seat. Joe brought them over a bottle and some boiled eggs. Mandy reached for an egg. Dan hit the platter, causing them to fly to the floor. "No food for you. I hate a fat woman."

Jim suddenly appeared in the doorway of the saloon. He stood tall and confident. "Dan Clocker!" he yelled as Dan jumped up and drew his gun. But Jim fired first, and Dan fell dead at Mandy's feet.

Mandy stood looking down at the dead man on the floor, as in a daze. "Why did he want to kill you, Jim?"

After glancing down at the body, Jim made his way over to Mandy, put his arm around her shoulders, and gently led her out the door and up to Doc's office. "Who knows? Probably, he was gunning for the law and not me specifically."

Later that day, Jim stood alongside a fresh grave in Boot Hill. He looked over the resting place of the man he killed and asked himself why.

Jim visited Mandy at Doc's office. He stayed with her when he was off duty. By the time she recovered, there was no doubt in anyone's mind that Mandy was indeed Jim's girl. That is, everyone except Mandy and Jim.

Love

Amanda's job kept her busy all the time. She would sit in for a dealer who was otherwise occupied, hustle drinks, sew dresses, and deal with dissatisfied customers. Amanda rarely had time for herself. She was tough, both with the girls and with the cowboys. She seemed to have a knack for controlling everything and anything that happened in her saloon. If she had a weakness at all, it was when that marshal who had her attention came into the bar. Those were the times she became distracted. It was his job to check the saloons for trouble several times throughout the night. Even the out-of-town cowboys noticed how the marshal hardly ever bothered to look directly at Mandy while every other man followed her around like a dog in heat.

Amanda would find herself watching for him, hoping no one would notice. She would watch the clock. Her heart would race as the time for his arrival would approach. Night after night, she would kick herself because she could not stop herself from staring at him. Just looking at him gave her an ecstatic feeling. She found him so handsome with his curly light-brown hair and large ice-blue eyes! She was floored! When the marshal was in town, she would take care to do up her hair differently and wear the best of her dresses.

He knew she was there, but every day, he would be so engrossed in keeping the peace and making sure no one was cheated with watered-down drinks or in the card game that he hardly seemed to take notice of her. Amanda stood on the Long Tree balcony for hours on end just to get a glimpse of him. Sometimes she would keep peeping out the window so that she could see him riding down the street on his bay horse. She would spot him heading out of town on marshaling business, and her heart would skip a beat. The rest of the time, she would just sadly retreat to her bed for some well-deserved rest or find some other work that needed doing.

As days passed and things remained the same, slowly and gradually, he started noticing that she stared at him all the time, when in the bar or in any shop. One day, Amanda was in the local shop when he came in. She turned around and, as usual, started staring at him. He was standing opposite her in that red shirt and brown vest he always wore, when suddenly a lot of people came in between them. She could see just one-half of his face and caught him staring at her with one eye! Amanda was shocked as it was so sudden and at the depth with which he was staring at her. It was not the lust of a cowboy fresh off the trail. There was admiration and tender love in those eyes! She left the store feeling elated but very shy. That look would remain in her mind for the rest of her life. In the long lonely nights to come, she would think of that look to comfort herself.

Amanda and James started spending more time together. Rumors started to fly. At first, the good men from Dodge felt the marshal should not be spending so much time at the Long Tree drinking, as he would not be able to shoot straight if the occasion should arise where his gun was needed.

One day, a group of outlaws rode into Dodge. James had been in the Long Tree all day and half the night. James staggered a little as he answered the outlaws' call. He stood alone in the street facing five well-armed, seasoned highwaymen. The huge marshal looked small as the morning sunrise caught his eyes. His marshal's star gleamed, giving the outlaws a good target. James, bold as brass, yelled, "I have paper on at least two of you! I am going to hold the rest till I can check on you all! That's the way to the jail!" He nodded. The five outlaws laughed at him. James's resigned voice turned sad. "Make your play."

The good men of Dodge saw one of the outlaws pull his gun. They never saw James pull his, but when the smoke cleared, all five men lay dead on the street. After that, there was no more talk of James being too drunk to carry a gun.

Then the gossip began that James was trading special favors in exchange for time with a shady lady. Closing the Long Tree for a week after a dealer was found to be cheating squashed those rumors. The local parson denounced keeping time with the ladies of the night. Although there were numerous gambling houses in Dodge, he specifically targeted the Long Tree. From the pulpit, looking at James as he spoke, he went so far as to name Mandy as an instrument of the devil sent to earth to defile the good name of Dodge City. James did not care. He knew in his heart that the parson was wrong.

Amanda was also feeling the heat. The good ladies of Dodge talked loudly about her corrupting the morals of the young marshal. Amanda became the town joke. The cowboys sang, "Mandy really handy when the marshal wants some candy. She makes him feel dandy when she brings him brandy. She gets a little dirty and acts a little flirty. Marshal gets nervy because she is so curvy."

Amanda and James felt it best to just ignore these goings-on. This was easier for James than Amanda. No woman enjoys being the town joke. She comforted herself with the dream that someday James would give up his badge and they would be married and have a family.

The young marshal, in an effort to control the wide-open town, started cracking down on the saloon owners. He made and enforced all kinds of laws. He started holding the saloon owners responsible for drunken cowboys who had a mind to shoot up the town. On the other hand, he made the cowboys who felt the need to break up the saloon pay for the damages. The Long Tree seemed to be hit hardest with the marshal's new laws. He no longer allowed the delivery wagons to block the street while delivering supplies to the Long Tree. The saloon was required to be closed by four in the morning, unless the herds were in town. The saloon could not open on Sunday until after Sunday services. Worst of all, he actually caught Mandy cheating while dealing at the poker table one night. In response, he closed the saloon down for a full week and would no longer let her deal cards at all. He enforced the prostitution license law at the Long Tree and still refused to sell one to Mandy.

To tell the truth, Mandy was not overly upset with the new laws. She was kind of tired of dealing and had stopped entertaining months before. She was also kind of happy for the extra sleep on Sunday but was displeased with the law whereby no working girl was allowed on the street before five. It was a law made so the decent ladies would not have to look at the women who entertained their husbands at night.

The Indians

Mandy was walking down Front Street when she spotted Mr. Favor, one of the regular trail bosses who was always nice to Mandy. Mr. Favor was in town to sell his herd. The herd was still about a week out yet. Mandy "accidentally" dropped her packages in front of Mr. Favor. He gallantly stooped and picked them up for her. "Thank you, kind sir. Come by the Long Tree for a drink on me," she said in a sweet Southern voice.

Mr. Favor smiled back. "Well, Miss Arness, I would not think of leaving town without stopping in to see you."

Mandy smiled and wondered how she was going to break the news to him that she no longer entertained. Later that day, Mr. Favor, Mandy, and two of Mandy's girls sat drinking at the Long Tree. It was decided between them that Mandy would bring the girls out to meet the cowboys before they hit town. For a price, of course. That way, the cowboys would be somewhat calmed down and would get into less trouble when they hit town. The girls would get acquainted with the cowboys, ensuring a good run at the Long Tree when the herds hit Dodge. The girls were agreeable as well. The plan was put into action.

Miss Mandy and Mr. Favor sat up in front of the wagon. The girls, ensconced in the back, were all dressed up in their working clothes, complete with large hats, feathers, and gloves. It was high noon when the wagon rolled down Front Street. The girls waved at all the men in town, to the disgust of the good ladies of Dodge. The good ladies complained to Hartford, the town's current deputy—a tall, skinny, all-right-looking man. He was the deputy but had no actual power to order the girls off the street. They were riding, not walking, so not breaking any laws. Besides, he was thoroughly enjoying the show. The girls gaily threw him some poker chips as they passed, him being a steady customer and all.

Two hours down the hot dusty trail, Mr. Favor stopped by a small bubbling stream flowing into the river so the women could get freshened up. Mandy found the place beautiful with crystal clear water and not a cloud in the azure sky. Yet in spite of all the beauty, she seemed to feel uneasy. Perhaps it was the stillness of the leaves or the lack of birds singing. Mandy was anxious to move out and was glad when Mr. Favor yelled, "Load up!" even though the girls protested. Mandy had just climbed onto the wagon when she heard the howling yell of an Indian brave. The sound made the hairs at the back of her neck stand up, and a cold dread dropped into her stomach. Within seconds, the band of Indians was upon them. Mr. Favor drew his six guns and was able to take out four of the savages before he was hit himself and fell off the wagon, dead. Mandy quickly pulled out her Sharps four-barrel twenty-two rimfire derringer that was concealed in her purse and her muff pistol from her stocking.

Knowing the small four-barrel Sharps was not a long-range weapon, she waited until a buck got close and grabbed for her. She then fired all four barrels into his chest. The Indian dropped lifelessly to the ground.

Mandy jumped off the wagon but saw the Indians were all around them. She ran the short distance to the river, but the bottom of her long Victorian dress absorbed the water, making running almost impossible. A buck easily overtook her in the middle of the swift-flowing river. She fired the second derringer. The four-barrel single-action derringer had a revolving firing pin. Unloading all thirty-two rimfire, she slid the four barrels forward to reload. Holding the small gun under her chin, she fired all four barrels. The derringer misfired. Before she could reload, a buck was on her. He grabbed hold of her and pushed her head under the water. Letting her up just long enough to keep her alive, he then dunked her under again. Pulling her by the hair, he dragged her over to the shore.

The buck then dumped her on the shore, thinking the fight had been taken out of her. He miscalculated. She jumped up pulling his knife and stabbed him in the leg. He hit her several times before overcoming her. This time, he took no chances and securely tied her spread eagle between two trees. The buck claimed her as his own. Cutting her dress laces, he then wiped his blood from his knife onto her exposed body. He took her laces to make a band for his head, then danced around chanting while cutting a piece of her dress with every turn. Mandy shivered at the cold and the knowledge of what was going to happen to her.

The other girls put up a good fight, but being outnumbered, it was to no avail. Mandy closed her eyes as tight as she could so she would not see her girls being gang-raped. She could block out the sight, but the sounds of their screams still reached her ears. She was about to give up all hope when she heard those words that gave her a glimmer of hope: "Fire, water."

Mandy had brought along on the wagon a pony keg of beer and a case of whiskey. Indians had only limited exposure to alcohol, and therefore, most had a low tolerance. This group of Indians was no exception. The buck who had been dancing around her stopped and went over to investigate. Shortly, he returned with a bottle in hand. She braced herself for the worst, but he was so busy dancing around and drinking that eventually he fell flat on his face. Mandy had fully expected the Indians would succumb to the booze quickly but was surprised at just how fast the buck became inebriated. Perhaps the lack of blood was a factor. At any rate, the buck did not bother her after he started drinking.

Her girls, however, were not that lucky. They were all gang-raped and beaten. Late in the night, things finally settled down. As morning crept over the hill, it found the girls still awake. By this time, most of the Indians were either in a drunken stupor or passed out. In their inebriated state, the Indians neglected to tie up their captives. The women released Mandy, and they all ran for the woods.

Back in Dodge, Jim got word that Mandy and a group of girls left Dodge in a wagon bound for the trail herders' camp. Recognizing the danger both from the cowboys and the Indians, Jim loaded up. Harford saw him getting an extra gun. Without a word, Harford also saddled up and joined him.

Although they had made their escape, the women were not yet safe. The ladies had little protection from the elements, as the Indians had cut up most of their clothing and had burned their shoes and stockings. As the girls ran, the brush slashed through their tender skin, and rocks cut into their feet. Along with their other injuries, the ladies left a blood trail that even a drunken Indian could follow.

Mandy, knowing the Indians would soon be after them, yelled, "Get in the water! They cannot track us in the water." Two of the girls were afraid of the Arkansas River as it was cold and swift. They were not swimmers. They felt that if they entered the river, they would drown. They made for the hills instead. Mandy yelled after them, "The Indians are good trackers! They will find you! If you must go, head for the cowherds! The cowboys will protect you!"

The Indians were occupying the area between the women and Dodge City. At the river, the girls debated whether to head upstream or down. Downstream would lead them into the hands of the Indians. But swimming upstream against the current would be very taxing as the current was so swift. So downstream they went. At least the cold water brought some relief from the pain of their injuries. As the sun rose higher in the sky, the water warmed. The group of tired women eventually found themselves in a warm pool of low-current water. The calm water had an occasional ripple. Surrounding the river was a beautiful variety of trees. Birds passed overhead, shadowing the deep-blue sky. Everything seemed peaceful. The women, being in the water for several hours, were now weary, waterlogged, and sunburned. Spotting a break in the steep and muddy banks of the large river, the women headed toward shore. They waded through pondweed as buzzing insects feasted on them, minnows darted about, and dragonflies circled their heads. About ten feet from shore, lily pads and some water lilies were growing up about three inches from the top of the water. Cattails also abounded. The beautiful setting was offset by the greasy mud squeezing up between their toes. Mandy's limbs seemed to weigh a ton as she exited the water and made her way through the spiky grass to the protection of the tree line. Once there, the battered women huddled together in their tattered clothes to find what protection they could from the elements and succumbed to much-needed sleep.

*****

The Indians awakened to find their captives missing. They were feeling the aftereffects from a night of heavy drinking. Rather than pursue the women, they decided to continue with their hunting. Knowing the tribe needed fresh meat more than the captives, they headed for the hills. As they started out for their hunt, they came across the two women who refused to go into the river, and they recaptured them.

*****

James and his deputy had been following the route the wagonload of women had taken. His fears intensified when he smelled smoke. Following the smoke, he found the mutilated body of Mr. Favor on the bank of a creek. Investigating the site, he found broken whiskey bottles, a barrel that once held beer, and remnants of destroyed dresses. This further intensified his fears. He found the trail of small bloody footprints, which indicated the women had gone that direction. The tracks were easy to follow. James was confused to find a trail indicating the Indians were going in a different direction. He found it hard to believe the women could escape from the Kawa, but the trails seemed to indicate just that. Recovering the women seemed more important than punishing the Indians. They followed the trail of small footprints.

Arriving at the banks of the Arkansas River, Harford said, "They would not try and swim the Arkansas River. The current can be pretty strong. Large sharp rocks and deep water make it dangerous."

James checked to see if they backtracked. Satisfied they didn't, he said, "They are in the river. They would rather fight the river than give up to the Indians. The current would stop them from going upstream. We'll head down. Stay as close to the bank as you can and keep your eyes peeled."

The ride was actually quite beautiful, with untouched virgin forest and cascading water. James reached Brown's Canyon with its awesome big waves and rocks leading into Dodge about sunset. He realized he must have passed the women somehow. There was no way the women could survive the canyon walls that go straight up. Harford chose to return to Dodge, feeling the women were lost to the river. James decided to take a ride back up the river, hoping the women got out somehow. He did not want to believe Mandy was dead. He would continue to look.

Harford said, "There's no way you are going to find them in the dark."

James looked determined. "I will camp along the creek and look for signs of them in the morning. Let me have your bedroll and blanket. When I find them, I will need them."

Harford thought James wanted to be alone, so he departed, knowing he would not be able to talk James out of searching. He wondered if James wanted the blankets for the purpose of burying the women.

James knew the Arkansas River well, having previously traveled its riverbanks in search of outlaws and renegades. He knew of only a few places the women could have safely gotten out of the river with the cover they thought they needed to avoid the Indians. He headed that way.

*****

Mandy awoke to see the majestic sun going down in a relentless array of red and purple. That was reflected in the captivating reflection of waves in the river. Puffy gray clouds hovered overhead as a thunderstorm raged off in the distance. Mandy woke the others, saying they needed to move to higher ground and find cover from the pending storm. Farther inland, they found a large white oak with limbs almost touching the ground. The girls huddled as close as they could to the trunk, giving them some protection from high winds and impending rain. A dinner of ripe pawpaws and tart graybark grapes they scavenged helped ease the women's aching stomachs.

None of them could hide the fear growing ever deeper in their souls. They were women who lived in the city, not accustomed to surviving out in the desolate countryside.

*****

James, still searching for the women, rode to the highest point he could think of. Sitting high in the saddle, he smelled the air. First, he smelled dust. Looking into the valley below, he realized a herd of buffalo was running north. The Indians were probably over there, hunting. James smelled the river—the smell of a swamp. He also smelled beef. Looking south, he saw the Faro herd bedded down for the night. Just beyond that was a campfire with several ramrods getting ready for some son-of-a-gun stew.

It was the smell that was coming from the northern direction that got his attention. It was the sweet scent of a wanting woman, the smell of a woman preparing herself to be gifted with a child. He also smelled the scent of fear. He leaned over and rubbed the neck of his trusted steed.

"Let's go get her," he said as he started to ride off the rock formation. It was getting late, and a storm was approaching. James knew the dangers of riding in the dark, but the full moon sufficiently lit the night sky. He let his horse find a trail, stopping occasionally to smell the air. Soon, he came upon the group of half-naked women huddled together.

Hearing the approaching horse, the women hid as best they could. Mandy alone stood up. She smelled something. It was not the sweaty, unwashed smell of the Indians. It was cured leather, saddle soap, and a man's body that she grew to know over the last several months. "It's James," she breathed as she ran out of their hiding place. "Jim...Jim!" she yelled as he approached.

Tears flowed freely as the women came from under the tree and ran toward him. Seeing this hero coming over the horizon was a kind of torture for the women, for he seemed to be riding very slow. But what a different and welcome kind of torture it was after what they had experienced. To them, the ordeal was finally over. The women ran and hobbled as fast as their injuries would allow them. Toward their hero they ran. It was a scene of sheer delight. The unforgettable ordeal, the nightmare, the uncertainty, the suffering was finally over.

James did what he could to ease their plight. He cut holes in the blankets he brought to cover the women's exposed bodies. He gave his shirt and second pair of pants to Mandy. James felt because of the pending storm and the night, which was growing even darker, they should stay put. He had some jerky, salt meat, dough gods, and long sweetening. He brought a prairie chicken he had shot, and he had some beans. Best of all, he had a flint stone. Knowing the Indians would likely not be coming after them this night, he said it would be okay to build a small fire.

Once the fire was built, the marshal addressed the women. "Ladies, there is no other help coming. We only have one horse. Two can ride at a time. We will switch every hour. The others will have to walk. It will not be easy. The woods are untamed, and the prairie is unforgiving. We must stay together. I do not want to spend any time hunting for someone who gets separated. You have lived through a terrible horror. I know you have the strength and stamina to make the trip."

The marshal dug a small hole and lined it with his raincoat. Using his coffeepot, he filled it with water and whiskey. "You ladies soak your feet in this. It will help." The water was cool and soothing. The women's nerves seemed to be cooled with the water. After each woman soaked her feet until the pain of walking through the brush abated, he then rubbed bacon on them to soften and protect them. Then using his fur-lined coat, with his knife he made each a pair of socks like moccasins. Perhaps it was hero worship, the moonlight, the warmth and light of the flickering fire, or just the relief from pain, but every woman fell adoringly in love with the tall handsome marshal that night. He was their hero, their savior. They cuddled up next to him like a moth flies to a flame. As he lay on the ground, four half-naked women were hugging on him. He smiled and wished his friends from Dodge could see him now.

There was one who was sitting by herself in the moonlight. Her blue eyes seemed to be brighter than the blue of the river. Her red hair was tangled—half up and half falling down over her naked shoulders. He could not help but wonder how it would feel if those lips—soft, luscious, and cherry red—would brush against his lips.

His mouth turned dry when one of the women said, "Don't worry about her. She can dry her own feet." It was then he realized he had dried all the feet of the other women, but not hers. He watched as she softly wiped her own feet with the well-used piece of pig fat. He wondered what her feet would feel like. He wished he had rubbed them. He watched as she made herself moccasins out of the leftover pieces of material, and he wondered why he feared helping her.

Off in the distance, a wolf howled at the moon. His howl was answered by another, then another. James pulled loose from the women, explaining he had to have his gun arm free in the event the wolf pack attacked. James put an extra log on the fire, and sparks flew high in the sky.

"We will have to post a guard. This fire must not go out. We will need more wood."

Amanda volunteered to help collect it. Piling the wood beside the fire, Amanda and James sat down for a much-needed cup of coffee.

"This is the best cup of coffee I have ever had," she said as her eyes sparkled with the light of the moon.

It was at that moment James knew he was hopelessly in love with her. Like the wolf, he wanted to howl at the moon with the hope she would howl back. No doubt she would have.

The silence of the night was deafening, broken by random strikes of lightning making its way to the ground off in the distance. James finally spoke. "Are you okay?"

Amanda smiled, her eyes reflecting the fire's intense light. "I will be… We do not have to tell the people in Dodge what happened to us, do we? It is none of their business."

James played with the fire. "I will have to make a report. You have my word no one in Dodge will read it." He softly put his hand on hers. "Your suffering, bad as it was, will help strengthen you."

She laughed a bold, healthy laugh that broke through the gloom of night. "I think I am strengthened enough. The challenges, difficulties, and painful situations can stop any time." What she said was not funny, yet James found himself laughing.

It started to rain, slowly at first. Then it became a real cloud buster. Try as they might, they could not keep the fire burning. Finally, they gave up and retreated to the tree. James made a makeshift tent using his bedroll. Although cold and wet, the women felt safe. James sat with his back against the tree, his gun at the ready. Mandy moved next to him. After a while, the storm moved off. The stars slowly appeared, twinkling through the dense clouds, and the night got quiet.

Then James heard the sound he had been dreading. One of the women began to sob, quietly. Soon, all the girls began to sob. It was gut-wrenching. All except for Mandy. Her sad eyes were filled with tears, but none escaped.

Hearing the crying women, James felt a sense of panic. He prayed for daylight. The morning sun reared up over the trees with an explosion of brightly colored light. The more James watched these women, the more he admired them. They made their way into his heart with a smooth reserve of strength. Through dense belts of brush and forest encumbered with fallen trees and boulder piles, across canyons, roaring streams, and sun-bleached fields, these women endured with both beauty and courage.

As they neared Dodge City, the thought of parading the half-dressed women down Front Street on their way back to the Long Tree did not sit well with him. He felt it best to detour to the Bender ranch first. It was located just outside of Dodge. Mrs. Bender was very happy to have some company and received them with open arms. She was dismayed at the state they were in and wanted to help. After a good meal, the women took a long bath and settled into a bed with clean sheets.

Mandy and James borrowed a wagon to go into Dodge to get clothing for the girls. On the way, James stopped the wagon under a shade tree. "Miss Mandy, when we get back to Dodge, would it be okay if I called on you?"

Mandy's heart jumped. Her arms ached for him. "You know you can come to the Long Tree anytime."

James took her tenderly in his arms. "No, not like that. Can I call on you as your man?" Very seriously, he went on. "Do you think you might want to change jobs? The thought of another man touching you drives me crazy."

Mandy rolled her eyes. "Jim, you have been the only one for almost a year now. I don't want any other man touching me."

James thought about that for a second. "What about Jack?"

Mandy looked embarrassed and very sad. "Jack has been a good friend for a long time. Sometimes we have slept together. He only talks about his wife. He feels the only way to keep the respect of his drovers is to get the head lady. James, even though we sleep together, we have never been together. He loves his wife."

Amazed, James laughed. "You mean Jack sleeps with you and only talks about his wife? You mean big old Jack is a phony? To hear him talk, he's God's gift to women."

Amanda was suddenly angry. "Don't you ever tell anyone that! Jack knows how I feel about you. He knows that if you ask me to be your woman, he would no longer be welcome in my bed. I always cater to the trail bosses, give them what they want. Mostly for free. That does not mean I have intercourse with them. Most of the time, they want the new girls for that. If one of them insists on having me, it is my job to go with him. If you are asking me to be your girl, only your girl, I will no longer do that."

James moved the horse and wagon on down the trail. "Being a marshal's woman is dangerous. I don't think we should tell anyone for your own safety."

Mandy's heart broke, but she was not yet willing to give up her new life as head lady. And she loved this man, so she agreed. "I have to tell Bill so he will know not to sell me to anyone. He is discreet. I think he will have no problem with it. He will probably tell them I have the clap." James laughed.

Dodge City came into view. James once again stopped the wagon. "Miss Amanda, may I kiss you?"

Amanda giggled. "Like you never did that before."

He brought her close. One arm was holding her tight around the waist, and the other was caressing her glorious hair. He held her for a few moments, their lips not touching, just feeling the breath on her face. The prolonged, delayed intimacy was fun, felt nice, and was a great way to be intimate without getting too intimate. Then he kissed her. It was deep and emotional, long, soft, searching, extended, and inferring there was more to come. At that moment, she was a bit afraid, shy, nervous, happy, excited, and hopelessly in love. "Oh my," she said as she turned every shade of red that morning.

The Comancheros

Upon returning to town, Mandy received the sad news. The two other girls who were with her had been recaptured by the Indians. A trader in human flesh came to Dodge and said he could ransom the girls for a price. He knew when and where the trading would take place. He could barter for the girls with merchandise the Indians desired. Mandy was not happy with the idea of dealing with this trader, but James said he was the only hope the girls had. Mandy went upstairs and dug under her mattress until she found a few hundred dollars she had hidden there. She took it back down to James and asked, "Will this be enough to buy the goods we need?"

James counted out the money and said, "It should be. I will bring you a receipt for the goods we buy. Sometimes the government will reimburse ransom money, but most likely, you will never recover one red cent of this."

Mandy determinedly shook her head. "I was responsible for the girls being taken. No price is too large for me to get them back."

Mandy wanted to go along on the trip to get the girls. The trader looked her up one side then down the other, smiled a knowing smile, and said he would welcome her along. At that, James knocked the trader off his feet. Then he took Mandy by the arm and told her, "You will do nothing of the kind. If you even go near the trading place, you will never come back. It is too dangerous for someone who looks like you do. Indians love a woman with red hair." He forcibly pushed Mandy back into the Long Tree and held her fast. "Bill, you keep ahold of her till we're far gone. It's for her own safety. We'll do what needs to be done."

The captured women would be slaves by now. James hated the idea of buying slaves but hated worse the very *idea* of slaves. James bought tools, cloth, flour, tobacco, livestock, coffee, and a keg of whiskey. He took a donkey and two fine horses. With two wagons of goods, he and the trader were on their way. Before he left, he had taken off his marshal's badge and handed it to Mandy to keep for him. "Dealing in human flesh should not be done while wearing a badge."

Amanda watched as they disappeared into the sunrise. They rode in silence, mostly because James had no use for this trader in human flesh. But the day at least was nice. A soft wind and warm sun made the ride kind of pleasant. They topped a hill that looked down on a peaceful valley. The trader stopped the laden wagon there and turned toward James. "I want to caution you, these people can be vicious. They are the worst men I have ever come across. You have to act like you're one of them, or the women you seek and we will never see the end of this day. They do not start the slave trade until late in the day. It gives men time to look over the crop."

James hated thinking of humans as a crop. It was distasteful. But he was ready to do what needed to be done to get those women back.

James was surprised by the jovial atmosphere when they entered the tent town. It seemed like they were going to a festival. All the men seemed to be cheerful, having a good time drinking and eating. James was further surprised when the trader told him it might take a week before the real bidding on the women would begin. During the waiting time, James blended in by participating in archery matches, wrestling bouts, and horse races. He kept his real identity a secret. Time was not moving fast enough for him. He was beginning to get restless when finally the real trading began. Initially, the trading was for foodstuffs—tobacco, pots, and metal points in exchange for the tribe's buffalo meat and robes. They traded manufactured goods (tools and cloth), flour, tobacco, as well as bread, hides, and livestock.

Meanwhile, James endured the mournful sound of wailing women and crying children. The children were roughly torn from their mothers' arms and offered up for trade as house slaves. Their crying mothers were offered as entertainment or as trade goods. James wanted to pull out his six guns and kill every one of these vile traders—Indian, Mexican, and White men alike. As far as he was concerned, they were all savages of the worst kind.

The trader was trying to make a deal for the women stolen from the area around Dodge. The Comanche had four women slaves taken from that area. The Comancheros had six. The women were brought before the men for their inspection. James thought he recognized three. He asked the price. The first woman, a redhead who had little to no marks on her, had an asking price of a keg of whiskey, ten pounds of coffee, and a mule. James said the price was too high, so a woman deemed of a lesser value was added to the deal. This woman's head, arms, and face were full of bruises and sores, and her nose was burned to the bone. Both nostrils were wide open and denuded of flesh. Although beaten when the woman tried to speak, the woman cried out, "Please, Mr. Russell!"

James then knew she was one of the women from the Long Tree. He quickly agreed to the deal. Others were brought before him. It was heartbreaking. When he was done trading, he had acquired a total of eight slaves. It was with great despair and deep sorrow James ended the trading as he had nothing left with which to trade. As it was, he had traded all their supplies. The trip back to Dodge was going to be a long and arduous one. He also wondered how these ravaged and scarred women would be treated in Dodge when they got back. Most men shared the view that it was a woman's duty to kill herself if taken by the Indians. They would not be easily accepted. His mind was full of worry as he left the trading place with the battered women.

The trader only rode with them halfway back. Having already been paid, he felt no need to return to Dodge. They parted ways. The marshal was never so happy to see Dodge come into view. He made camp just outside of town and waited until the cover of night. Then he slowly moved the wagon discretely into town through the darkened street to Doc's office. Doc treated the women with compassion. He did not have enough beds for all the women. He sent James over to get Amanda from the Long Tree.

James stood outside of the Long Tree looking over the batwing doors. He spotted Mandy to one side laughing with some cowboys.

The pangs of jealousy were churning in his stomach. He was about to go in and knock that cowboy into the middle of next week when she spun loose, pushing the cowboy back playfully. Spotting James, she exclaimed, "Jim, you're back!"

James entered the brightly lit saloon. In a lowered and somber voice, he said, "Doc would like you to come up."

Mandy grabbed her velvet triangular shawl, the one with the big red rose embroidered in it, as she hurriedly headed out the door. James could not help but think she was a sight as breathtaking as that big red rose. As they walked, James tried to warn her. "I traded all your goods and got both women. I just could not let those other women remain there. I brought back eight women altogether. I hated leaving the rest but had nothing left to trade except the wagon that we needed to make it back to Dodge and my gun. I could not sell them my gun. Amanda, it was worse than I imagined. They are a mess. Amanda, the girls' faces are all beat up. You need to brace yourself."

Mandy shook her head. "I am not a farm girl. I have seen some nasty things in my time. Back in New Orleans, I used to take care of the girls when they had a bad night."

James looked very sad. "It's the worst I have ever seen. Mandy, it is important you do not react to how bad they look. The only chance they have of recovering from this depends on you."

Mandy's years of working in a saloon paid off when she actually saw the poor women. No one could tell the emotional pain growing deep inside of her. She smiled as she said to them, "Hey, you gold-bricks. When are you figuring on coming back to work?" knowing full well these women would never work in a saloon again. In fact, they would never be able to find any kind of work, disfigured as they were. They would live their lives out as beggars, turned away by every man who looked at them.

These women had no future before them. Mandy felt the deep need to do something to help them cope. There had to be something. James agreed.

Mandy and James arranged to buy an abandoned farm from the state for the taxes owed on it. Some of the relatives and friends of the freed women were contacted and helped build a simple house, not wanting to have the women return to their homes. The women made this their home. The women survived by making jewelry, doing beading for the dress shop, and growing food for the Long Tree's free lunch. Mandy and Jim did most of the shopping for the farm as the women were scorned and made fun of when they entered the town. They at least had a place to live, a way to earn money, and each other.

James never forgot those other poor captive women he had to leave behind. Their faces haunted his dreams for the rest of his life. He repeatedly wrote letters and used all the power of the marshal's office to get the military to end the trade of captives. The Indians, having the idea of slaves as currency embedded in their society, were not willing to give up the practice. It would continue until the defeat of the nations.

A Little Help from Her Friends

Mandy, feeling the loss of wealth due to the expense of the trade for the captured women, told Bill she would start taking some clients of her own. Bill was jumping for joy, for many men had requested to purchase her favors. She felt bad about the prior promise she made to James, but a woman must look out for herself. Besides, he did not ask her to be his wife, she reasoned. The truth be told, in a nice way, he kind of asked her to be his exclusive whore.

Mandy was working hard day and night to recoup her losses. Bill knew she was only taking clients until her bank account improved. But it was taking a toll on her. She was sent two men a day who paid her top dollar, leaving her time to work in the bar at night. Then he sent her one rich client who paid double at closing time. Within a week, Mandy was showing signs of exhaustion. She was sick of the bar, sick of men, and, worst of all, sick of herself. The only thing that made this bearable was that James was out of town.

After kicking the previous night's client out of her bedroom, she wearily went downstairs for some much-needed coffee. Bill came over to her. "I have a special client who wants to buy your time for the entire week." Mandy did not like the sound of that. The best client was one who left as soon as he took his due. A client who wanted to stay over was likely to want more from her than she wanted to give. Or worse yet, he would fall in love with her and make a pest of himself. But the money was good, and she would be able to stop after this one special client.

"What did he ask for?"

Bill smiled. "Nothing special, just your time."

Everything inside Mandy warned her no. Sadly, her mouth said, "Yes." Mandy got a bath to relax herself, then went for a walk to get

103

some fresh air before her long week would begin. She wondered what this man would demand from her. She thought of the times in the past when men did unspeakable things to her. Slowly, she returned to the Long Tree. Might as well get this over with.

Entering the Long Tree, Bill called to her, "You have a client waiting in your room." Slowly, she walked up the long steep stairs and down the long narrow hall. Her door was cracked open. Slowly, she pushed open the large heavy door. Her heart sank.

"Oh, it's you." She felt worthless like a well-used, spoiled piece of beef. *No, no, no*, she thought. *I thought we were friends.*

He took her hand and led her to the bed. "I want you to put this on," he said as he handed her a long soft cotton sleeping shirt. "Let your hair down loose. Bill told you I bought your time for a week, didn't he?" She started to undress. "No, go behind the divider."

Mandy felt like crying. "Yes, Bill did tell me. What would you like me to do?"

He replied, "Come out. Now get into bed."

Mandy sighed and put on her best saloon-gal smile. "What's your pleasure, cowboy?" she asked, sticking her leg out the slit on the side.

He took on a commanding voice. "Get over here and get in bed."

She did as she was told. He bent down and covered her with a light blanket, then followed with a heavy quilt. "You have been looking very tired lately, and I know you have only been eating boiled eggs and pickles. So I bought your time so you can get some much-needed sleep. Now I am going back to my office. When I come back later, we will have a nice meal, and you will eat every-thing on your plate. Then you will go back to bed while I read my new medical book."

Mandy sat up. "You aren't going to…"

Doc smiled. "I never think of you that way. You're James's woman. You are my dear friend. This week, you don't leave this room. You sleep and eat and get your real smile back. Doctor's orders. I talked to Harford. James will be back the first of next week, so it's time for you give up this foolishness."

Amanda looked a little confused. "Can you afford this? Bill will want his cut."

Doc laughed. "Bill owes me a lot of money. He will never pay what he owes. I told him I wanted you to do something special so he would, in turn, pay you top dollar. I have done this before. He always pays good. You won't lose out. And I get something for taking care of all you girls. Besides, I get the pleasure of your company for a week."

Amanda did as her customer ordered and snuggled down under the soft quilt. It was blissful. By the end of the week, she had the color back in her cheeks and her old smile back. She quit entertaining and returned to be just a madam in the bar.

The Draft

Mandy looked up from the tedium of her books as Mr. Tomson walked into the bar. Mr. Tomson was an older hardworking sod-buster, who usually never came into the saloon this early in the month. She nodded politely. "Mr. Tomson, good afternoon. First drink is on the house."

Mr. Tomson smiled. "Thank you, Miss Mandy. But I was wondering if I could get some advice from you."

Amanda was surprised. "Sure, but I should warn you I know very little about cattle."

Mr. Tomson laughed. "I just paid off my farm. I bought supplies and seed for next year's crop. I am heading home to celebrate with the misses. I would like to buy her something as well in celebration. Some kind of lady thing. But I don't know what to get her. I have about $6 to spend."

Amanda turned to Sam. "Give him an extra drink on the house. Congratulations. That is surely something. You and your wife have worked hard all these years. I am glad to see it is paying off. In honor of your mortgage burning, I think I have a hat upstairs that does not fit me right. You can have it."

Mr. Tomson looked confused. "No offense, but Mary does not dress as fancy as you do, Miss Mandy."

Amanda winked. "Oh, it really is not my style. I think she will love it. I have a few other things she might like also. I will bring them down while you have another drink." With that, Amanda headed up the stairs.

Mr. Tomson turned to Sam. "I just wanted some advice."

Sam smiled. "Just take a look at the things. If you don't like them, she will not be insulted. She does have great taste."

Mr. Tomson finished his first drink. "Please tell Miss Mandy I will return shortly. I need to get my mail before the post office closes. Mary is hoping for a letter from her sister. We have not heard from her since this war started. I will be right back."

Amanda came back into the room and set a dress, hat, and some perfume on a table. James walked in just then and looked at the pile of pretty things. "Not another dance?"

Amanda laughed. "No, you're safe. I was thinking of giving these to Mary Tomson. They just paid off the farm and are going to have a celebration."

James tried to be diplomatic. "Mandy, you and Mary Tomson have different styles. I don't think…"

Amanda nodded. "You don't think. A woman likes to dress up once in a while. She would look great in this," she said as she gestured toward the dress. It was not a saloon-girl dress but a simple style made out of a better fabric.

Mr. Tomson walked back in as James held up the dress in question. "You got that right, Miss Mandy. But like I said, I only have about $6 to spend." Amanda got a box from the back and started packing the pretty dress into it.

"Like I said, I can't fit in this anymore. You would be doing me a kindness by taking it off my hands."

Mr. Tomson smiled. "Well, thank you, Miss Mandy. I normally would not take it, but the store is now closed. And I really wanted to take her something nice to celebrate."

James put some coins on the bar. "I hear you paid off the farm. Let me buy you a drink. Sam?" Sam was getting the drinks. "Did you hear from Mary's sister?"

Mr. Tomson fumbled through three weeks of mail. "No, but I got some letters that look kind of official. I am not much for reading. Miss Mandy, will you read them for me?"

Mandy nodded and opened up the first letter. She slid the official-looking letter out of the envelope and glanced at it. Frowning, she said, "Well, this must be some kind of mistake. It's a conscription, a draft notice, from the Confederate States of America. Sam, take a look at this." She handed the bartender the letter and opened the second one. "Well, this is your lucky day. You have been drafted by the United States of America as well."

Mr. Tomson grabbed the first letter. "This has to be a joke. I can't be drafted for the Confederates! I live in Kansas. I can't be drafted at all. I will be fifty next month!"

Sam looked concerned. "I hear the South is taking all able-bodied men from fifteen to fifty. The North is desperately hurting for recruits also."

James read over both letters. "Both look legal to me. The one from the Confederates I would think would be the less legal because Kansas voted to go with the North in 1861. Kansas had been an open territory since 1854, allowing each community to decide the issue of home rule and slavery for itself. But in 1860, by popular vote, Kansas became a free state, not to say that slavery does not go on. They just call it indentured servants now. How do you feel about home rule?"

Mr. Tomson, clearly agitated, downed a drink in one gulp. "I don't have time to decide everything for everyone. I have spent all my time just getting the farm to pay off. Never took sides on any of those fighting issues. How can they draft me? I never voted. I never stuck my nose into anyone's business. I just want to be left alone to grow things."

James rubbed his neck. "This puts me in a bad position. I think a person should have the right to fight for what he believes in, but if I was to hear of a person acting against the Union like joining the Confederates, I would have to arrest him for treason."

Mr. Tomson turned, stared at James, and grabbed the letters. "I best be getting home."

Mandy handed him the box for his wife.

"Thank you kindly," Mr. Tomson said. "I do not think we will be celebrating tonight."

Mandy smiled. "This madness cannot go on much longer. The war has to come to an end soon."

Mr. Tomson smiled weakly, then left.

James downed his drink. "It is worse than he thinks. The provost marshal is coming to Dodge tomorrow, bringing me a list of land that I am duty bound to acquisition for the army. It is just a guess, but the Tomson farm is in the path of the advancing army."

It took a few moments for Amanda to fully understand James's comment. Then it hit her like a hot poker. "Oh, James, you can't!"

James looked deep into her eyes. "I can do as I am told or resign. Everyone is resigning. I do not know where I can get another job. Maybe I can be a cattle drover or become a trapper."

Later that night, Amanda stared up from her soft goose-feather-filled mattress and watched as James slowly opened the door and quietly removed his boots and socks. He hung his guns and hat on the gun rack. Then he slumped onto her settee, laid his head back, and closed his eyes. She smiled. He looked so handsome and troubled. She thought about joining him, then thought better of it. Even a strong man like James needed some peaceful time. Her room was the only safe place he had. No one ever shot at him there. Well, not lately.

After some time, James opened his eyes and saw her looking at him. "Hi."

She smiled. "Hi. Are you okay?"

He looked up at the ceiling. "I wrote the war department, telling them I quit my job. I have no idea what I am going to do now. I just could not take everything away that all those homesteaders have. After all the work they put into their farms, all the insurmountable obstacles they have endured. It is their life—their livelihood. The Union army has many hardships also—lack of food, inadequate clothing. They're fighting with nothing to fight with. What's your opinion?"

Amanda noticed an envelope marked "War Department" in his hand. She got up, fetched a bottle of whiskey, and went to sit with him. "I never wanted to discuss the war with you. I try not to get involved. I do not know about home rule. A town should be able to spend their own tax money on what the town needs. But a central government is a strong government with the resources to protect and provide for the members of that government. I do not understand the difference between a territory and a state, as to which one is better. I was born in the South. I know the Confederates are fighting for the rights of the South, for their way of life and self-government. The men in the South are defending their homeland.

"As for the issue of slavery, the plantations need workers. In the North, I hear men are forced to spend fifteen hours a day in the mines and are paid a script to buy things at the company store, leaving them no money at the end of the week. I have heard of men being hung for missing a production schedule and gunned down when they felt the mines were too dangerous to work in. In the South, the Negros are provided for by the plantation owner. Keeping them healthy is in the plantation owner's best interest. In the North, children are put to work as young as four years old in the mines and factories. They work all their lives in debt to the owners. The owners provide food, housing, and clothing. The owners tell the men when to work and how long. Kind of like the plantation owners.

"Lincoln talks a lot about freedom of men, yet he himself owns slaves. He believes Negros should not have the same rights as White people, but he wants colonization of the Negros in one place so the Whites can keep control of them. He is interested in stopping the Southern rebellion to save the Southern dollars. Therefore, the loss of about one hundred thousand lives is on his head.

"General Lee is a freedom believer. He inherited slaves from the death of his father but freed them. He is against slavery and is just fighting to save his homeland." She took a drink and moved closer so he could feel her soft body.

"I, myself, have been sold many times. I was forced to do things I did not want to for the amusement of men. There was a time when I had no say about anything in my life. I was told what to eat, where to go, and how to dress. I was not even given the right to speak, and I was beaten if I did not perform well enough. I met a lot of people. Some of them liked that way of life—not having to make any decisions. It was not for me. As to war, I think it is truly tragic. No one will win. It is just a loss that will plague us for generations to come."

She kissed him softly and looked deep into his sad eyes. "As for your job, you have to do what you think is best. You're a strong man. You can get other work if that's what you decide."

James rubbed his head. "For someone who does not want to talk about war, you seem to have a lot to say."

Mandy gently put her head on his shoulder. "That's because I do not understand it at all."

James sighed and hugged her tight. "Amanda, the Union army often takes over the biggest building in town for a headquarters. If they come to Dodge, this building is a good location with access to the railroad and the river. If they decide to occupy this building, I want you to promise me you will not fight them. Do as they say and keep out of sight as much as you can for your own safety. They will take all your supplies and give you a government script. That might be good after the war is over. It is not a good thing, but you might get some money back."

She moved in tight. "Yeah, about three cents on the dollar or less," she drawled.

He held her, wishing he would never have to let her go. He prayed this night would not end and he would never have to leave this room.

The War Ends

Jim looked at her calendar. It was April 9, the last day he would be a marshal. He wondered how she would feel about him being a smelly trapper or a dusty cow puncher. His thoughts were interrupted by the sounds of the local church bell pealing.

Mandy woke up to the ringing. "Is this Sunday?" The quiet was broken by the mine siren going off, and then the train started ringing its bell and blowing its siren. Then noise of men and women and children shouting rose up from the street.

James went to the open window, leaned out, and yelled down, "Hey, what's going on?"

Mr. Jones waved his hat. "Lee surrendered. The war is over!" he gaily shouted.

Mandy jumped up and ran into James's arms. "Did he say it was over?"

James grabbed her and swung her around. "It is over!"

The noise from the street got louder as everyone in town grabbed whatever noisemaker they could find to celebrate the new-found peace.

Mandy said, "I have to get dressed. You better get down there. If the partying gets too bad, you may have to protect the town... marshal."

James strapped on his gun belt. "The town be damned. Let's celebrate!"

She went to the stair rail, leaned over, and yelled, "Sam, tap a keg and open the doors!" They sang, danced, and partied the day away until most could no longer stand up.

The party raged on through the night and into the next day. Everyone was happy. James had his hands full, keeping the party under control. He went easy on most of the unruly partying cowboys, mostly because he also felt like joining them and painting the town red. Mandy was also very busy handing out a multitude of drinks. It ended up being three days of solid partying. Then the reality of the cost of this unforgiving war sank in as they remembered the dead and the victims.

Every family had lost someone, but on the same note, almost every family had a child coming of age. Their young lives were spared by General Lee's decision to go against orders. With his own name, Lee had signed the documents that saved countless lives. It seemed the Southern rebels' as well as the Union loyalists' resolve had been weakened by the four years of bloodshed. The end of a useless dirty war was a time to celebrate with hope for the future. That is not to say James did not have to ride herd on few drunken cowboys set on refighting the war in the confines of the local bars.

A telegram arrived stating a troop train of returning soldiers was to be mustered out at Fort Dodge. They would be arriving on April 14. The telegram was signed only "We are coming home."

This information brought a new round of partying. It was agreed the town would have a celebration of thanksgiving in the town square on April 15, 1865. All the merchants and shop owners were participating.

Amanda and James were almost the only ones left who were still busy setting up for the next day's celebration. It was late, and Amanda was about to return to the Long Tree to relieve Sam when Tom, the telegraph operator who was keeping the office open late to receive word of returning soldiers, came running down the street. Amanda could tell by the distressed look on his haggard face that something bad had happened. He ran straight up to James and handed him the telegram.

James read the note and stood for a moment in stunned silence. He then yelled, "This town is under martial law! Everyone, return to your homes and stay there until you hear from my office. All businesses are now closed and will not reopen until you get word from me." Then he turned and headed toward the telegraph office.

Amanda hurriedly ran after him. "What is it?" she queried.

James turned to look at her with fear in his eyes. "Go home and stay there. It is a mistake. It has to be a mistake." Looking at Tom, he said, "No one talks about this until it is confirmed. Tom, you come with me."

Everyone was startled but did what the law instructed. They all wondered what had happened, but no one could have imagined the words that would reach them in the morning. Mandy walked alone through the dimly lit, deserted, dusty streets, distraught that Jim did not trust her enough to confide in her what happened. It must be something serious for him to behave as he had. Arriving at the Long Tree, she ordered it closed. The remaining cowboys asked her why, but she had nothing to tell them.

A sense of pending doom gripped James as he anxiously sat in the telegraph office. It could not be true. He read the telegram again. "President Lincoln stabbed near death." *How could this be?* James questioned how anyone could even get close enough to stab President Lincoln. *If it is true, what would happen now?*

Tom asked, "If the president was assassinated by a Southerner, would the war start up again?"

The question made James feel sick all over. Dodge had not been a battleground for the war. Yet many in Dodge served as Confederates and many as Yankees. Border ruffians, abolitionists, and Jayhawkers made Dodge a powder keg. It did not bode well. Seconds ticked by like hours while he awaited further word.

Amanda stood at her window above the saloon getting madder and madder. She paced back and forth. She needed to know what had upset James so terribly. Finally, she could not take not knowing any longer. She determinedly left her room, strode down the staircase, and ran across the street. James was happy to have her with him, but he was angry she went against his orders. He was about to demand she go back to the bar when word from the war department came clicking through the telegraph: "President Lincoln has been shot, believed mortally. All law and military officials are on alert. Assassins escaped."

Amanda immediately burst into tears. "No, oh my God, no. James, what now?"

The marshal was trying to stay cool and composed. He said, "It depends on if he survives or not. If he dies, I guess Johnson is president."

The telegraph began to tap again. "Attempted assassination United States Secretary of State William H. Seward."

Tom looked glumly over at James. "It's an attempt to overthrow the Union government. They want to throw us back into war!" he exclaimed. He slumped forward and put his head in his hands.

James stood frozen for a second, then turned to Amanda. Hoarsely, he instructed her, "Go get Parson Wilson and Mr. Lewis, the reporter. Talk to no one else. Bring them directly here. The people will have to be told."

Amanda jumped up to do as she was bid. She returned shortly with both the men.

Mr. Lewis was irate. "What's so important you've got to roust a person out of bed at this ungodly hour?" he demanded.

Then Parson asked, "What is it? How can I help?"

James offered them coffee and was about to tell them of the attempts when the telegraph began clicking again.

Tom sadly announced, "It's from the war department. President Abraham Lincoln died this morning at twenty-two minutes after seven." All in the telegraph office were in a state of shock.

James said softly, "Parson, please go ring the church bell. Harford, raise the flag to half-mast." He did not have to say anything to Mr. Lewis, for he had run out of the office and was halfway back into the printer's office. James called after him, "Hey, be careful. We do not want to incite any reprisals. There has been enough bloodshed."

Mr. Lewis called back, "I will report only the facts."

Hearing the church bell ringing, the confused townspeople started filing into the streets. News of the death of the president was revealed and spread like wildfire. Amanda felt sick, tired, and scared. Everyone became silent and sad that the civil war had claimed another man's blood.

James had reason to be concerned about people's reactions. Many openly mourned while others celebrated. Many of the people just did not believe it was true. Later that night, James stopped by the Long Tree to get some much-needed coffee. "I cannot believe these people. A man is dead. That is never a reason to celebrate."

Amanda explained it. "President Lincoln was a symbol of a war that ripped us all apart, and he was the winner. A lot of people are still feeling the loss. They need someone to blame, and they blamed him. Many have lost everything they had for a failed cause."

James shook his head. "Even so, the gleeful celebration of a man's death is shocking."

Amanda took a long drink of coffee. "Do you think this will change the course of the war? I mean produce anarchy within the Yankees?"

James stood up and began pacing. "That is why I need to keep a lid on Dodge. If people are of a mind to refight this war, I do not want Dodge to be a battleground. I personally think more bloodshed will help no one. Please stay inside where you are safe. This could erupt in a violent confrontation at any time."

Mandy stood up. "You must wonder about the will of God, letting such a terrible event happen on Good Friday. Do you know if they are going ahead with Easter services? I donated a box of candles that no one has come to pick up. I thought about taking them over to the church."

James moved toward the door. "No, don't go to the church. If they have the celebration, I will come and get the candles. I need to know you're safe."

Mandy smiled. "Okay. You know I can take care of myself."

James looked very sad. "You don't understand. This is a powder keg situation. This could be Lawrence, Kansas, all over again. People do not act rationally in times like this. It is not safe for anyone to be out on the street."

The realization struck Amanda with terrifying fear. "No. Jim, God, no! Well, I intended to close for Easter anyway—not much business."

James cautioned, "I am asking everyone to keep businesses closed and to stay off the street as much as possible, until we find out more of what's going on. I will put a curfew in place. The world seems to be in a state of shock, and everyone seems to be going crazy. I fear what will happen when the shock subsides. Mandy, pass the word that I will have to arrest anyone openly praising the president's death. I do not believe the killers could get this far, as the railroads and stage lines are being watched. But anyone giving comfort to the assassins will be arrested. I will stop back when I can."

The twelve days to come were filled with anxiety and uncertainty. Across the nation, a lot of Confederate leaders who were left to return to their homes were now rounded up and jailed on conspiracy charges. James was sent a list of those in Dodge to be arrested. He was surprised to see Amanda's name on the list. When he asked the war department why, he was told she was a Southern spy who lived for a time at a Southern camp and was a one-time friend of Mary Suratt.

James instructed the telegraph operator to keep quiet about the list. "If you tell anyone about this list, I will have you arrested and charged with warning conspirators." He then put the list in his pocket. He detained no one. He only visited all on the list and warned them to stay in their homes for their own safety. "To try to flee would be met with your arrest for treason."

The newspaper summed it all up with a quote from Jefferson Davis: "If it be done, it is better it was done well… For an enemy so relentless in the war for our subjugation, we could not be expected to mourn. Yet in view of its political consequences, it [the death of Lincoln] could not be regarded otherwise than as a great misfortune to the South."

Amanda was somberly draping the Long Tree in black when James walked up. "I need to talk to you. Now."

Amanda was a little shaken by his tone of voice. She couldn't imagine what he was upset with her about. "What's the matter, Jim?"

He grabbed her arm and pushed her none too gently into the Long Tree. He whispered into her ear, "Get upstairs. This is bad."

Mandy was upset at his ungentlemanly treatment of her and was getting madder. She didn't understand it. She stopped at the bottom of the stairs. "James!" Her words were cut off as James pushed her toward the stairs.

"Get up there!" he said with gritted teeth.

Realizing something was seriously wrong, she obeyed. In the privacy of her room, he took her in his arms and held her like he was about to lose her. "Mandy, I have orders to arrest you. They say you are friends with Mary Surratt."

Mandy struggled to get loose. "Who?" she asked with confusion.

James let go and sat down heavily on the settee. With his head lowered, he said, "The lady who helped kill Lincoln."

Amanda looked stunned. "What? Who?"

James looked at her like a marshal would look at a suspect. He repeated, "Mary Surratt."

Amanda sat down next to him. She gazed directly into his blue eyes. "I don't know any Mary Surratt."

James sounded concerned. "What about John Booth? Do you know him?"

Amanda definitively shook her head. "No. Not that I recall."

James sounded a little less condescending. "No one can say they saw you with Mary Surratt? You never met her?"

Amanda thought of all the girls she had met over the years. "You know I worked in a few houses over the years. Girls came and went. Most of them used false names. To my knowledge, I have never met her. Ever."

Just then, a rock came sailing through the window of the Long Tree, shattering the glass. James grabbed his gun. "I need time to stop this from going any further. I am going to lock you in your room. You stay in. Pack a bag with only what you need for a few days. If I send you word, get out of Dodge fast. Go find Hank in the nations. He will hide you with the Indians. I will leave a buggy in the back. Use the back stairs. Tell no one. I will come when it is safe." And he was gone.

Accused

Mandy sat forlornly on the bed. How could anyone think she had anything to do with the killing of the president of the Union? That was just ludicrous. She packed a bag and slid it far under the bed so it would not be seen by anyone who entered the room. The noise from the street below was getting louder and rowdier. She heard things being broken in the saloon. She took a deep breath and walked over to the window. She made sure to stand behind the heavy drapes so no one could see her. She saw James holding off the town with just one six gun and the pride, confidence, and fortitude of a person in the right. Although up against many, he was still a symbol of authority.

Mandy thought about life with the Indians if she had to flee. No matter how hard she tried to picture it, one thing she knew with absolute certainty was she did not have the temperament to be a squaw. Walking behind a man's horse, chewing on raw buffalo hide for him was not for her. She went to the closet and got out her old street walker dress. Maybe she would go to Mexico instead and walk the streets of Laredo. Peering into the looking glass, she thought, *There is nothing worse than an old whore.*

She then thought of James. What would the good people of Dodge do if they did not get a pound of her flesh? James believed strongly that the law would protect the innocent, and that was her. *This is the dumbest thing I have ever done*, she thought as she dressed in her fanciest dress. She put on a very large fashionable hat complete with feathers. She then descended the staircase to the street to stand courageously alongside her man. The mob was taken aback.

One of her regulars yelled, "She will do anything for money!" He picked up a stone and prepared to throw.

James moved in front of her. "You throw that, and I will blow your head off!" he warned.

Amanda held her head high in the air and did the saloon-girl strut as she sashayed her way across the street and into the local jail. James followed, his gun at the ready.

James did not place Amanda in a jail cell. Instead, he held a chair for her and got some coffee. "What are you doing?" he asked.

Amanda looked as if she might cry. "I have been around the block, seen everything, done everything. The only place I was ever happy was in Dodge. I must face this here. I trust you and love you. If I am to die, let it be here." Amanda got up and slowly walked to the last cell. From the barred window, she watched the mob push into the Long Tree, her home. She watched as Sam was thrown violently into the street.

James did not lock the cell. "I will put a stop to that."

Amanda turned and looked at him. "Let them have their fun. Once all the booze is gone, they will no longer have any reason to hang me, except they love a good hanging. James, if you could please protect my girls?"

James forced a smile. "The only time I have ever been happy was with you. I have got to go. They plan on tearing the town apart. I am going to lock the front door to keep them out. Amanda, if they break in…" He looked her in the eyes. She could see his fear, sadness, and regret. He lowered his head toward her.

She smiled and touched his hand softly. "Marshal, you are slipping. You forgot to remove my weapons. I have my derringer. They will not take me."

James looked profoundly into her eyes, grabbed her hand, and held it tight. The sound of shouts and the windows at the Long Tree being broken jolted them back to reality. James turned and headed toward the door. He glanced back, smiled, and was gone.

Amanda heard the slight sharp sound of the lock on the front door over the sounds of the street. The air seemed to go out of the room. She sank dejectedly to the stone floor. In despair, she heard her long dead mother's voice: "Stand up, girl. You will soil your dress. You've done nothing wrong, so don't act like you have."

Amanda looked up and saw the opaque willowy figure of her mother. "Please, Mommy, come take me home," she cried, even as she knew it was not real.

Her mother reached out with her soft white arms. "I cannot, but I will sit with you. Do not fear. It will be okay."

Amanda curled up on the cot, held safely in the sweet arms of her departed mother. She listened as the mob destroyed everything for which she had worked so hard. After the noise abated, the Long Tree was still standing, but every window and door was broken. The stools and tables lay broken in pieces in the street. Waving high on the town flagpole were Amanda's red silk bloomers. Men were sleeping it off in the street and on the sidewalk. Beside them were bottles of high-end booze. She did not know where her girls were. The scariest thing to Amanda was that she could not see James anywhere. She worried something had happened to him. Shrinking down, she again curled up in her mother's arms. She felt safe and warm. She soon fell asleep.

Amanda was awakened by something hitting the outside door. She pulled out her derringer, put it in her mouth, and stood at the ready. The door creaked as it slowly opened.

James fell through in the doorway, and Amanda rushed to his side. "Close the door," James whispered through swollen lips. Amanda had to move his very heavy legs so she could slam the door. "Board it!" James pointed at a solid wooden plank by the door. Amanda placed the heavy board in the appropriate slots.

"Get a shotgun," James instructed and gestured over toward the gun rack. With a loaded shotgun in hand, Amanda pulled the heavy marshal away from the door and looked for injuries. She jumped when she heard someone else pounding at the door.

"Hey, you in the jail, let me in. It's Doc." She ran back to the door and lifted the heavy board to let Doc in. He was already at James's side as Amanda replaced the barricade.

The marshal's injuries were, for the most part, superficial. "No broken bones. I think you will live unless the good townspeople decide to hang you," Doc said as he packed up his bag. Mandy breathed a sigh of relief.

Amanda stayed put in the jailhouse as James, with the help of soldiers from Fort Dodge, tried to retake the city. They received word that the assassin Booth was killed and eight others were arrested. This news, along with the Long Tree running out of booze and the needs of the men to work their farms, somewhat cooled off the uprising in the city.

As things died down slightly, Doc brought a newspaper into the jail. Amanda got him some coffee. Doc softly took her hand. "Looks like we have more bad news. It seems they are going to try anyone accused of the conspiracy by military tribunal rather than the civil court."

Amanda took a long drink of her coffee. "I don't understand."

Doc explained, "At the time of Lincoln's death, the war was not yet over. Neither the fall of Richmond nor Lee's surrender at Appomattox ended the war. Sherman is still fighting Joe Johnston in the Carolinas. The war is not over."

Amanda thought about that for a while. "So why does it matter if it is a civil court or a military one?"

Doc again tried to explain. "A military trial has wider rules of evidence than a civil trial. Prisoners are not allowed to testify on their own behalf."

Soon after, a major from Fort Dodge along with some soldiers entered the jail and gave James a piece of paper ordering him to turn over the prisoner, Amanda Arness. James initially refused, but the soldiers leveled their guns at him. The soldiers put shackles on Amanda's legs and wrists. She smiled waveringly but reassuringly at James as a soldier put a hood over her head. He dragged her out onto the street and callously threw her in the back of a military wagon. The regiment drove her slowly through the street so everyone could gaze upon the traitor, hooded and shackled. At the fort, she was placed in the stockade still hooded and chained.

James tried but was not permitted to see her. He set out to hire her a lawyer, but no one wanted to take on the job. He ended up with an inexperienced kid just out of law school, the only one willing to take the case. He need not have bothered.

After two weeks of intensive interrogation at the fort, Amanda continued to maintain her innocence. She told them she was an entertainer who was neutral in the war. She told them that being on anyone's side was unprofitable to her. The soldiers could not afford her, and she did not know nor did she want to know the people she entertained. She admitted to taking the money from the dead in the stagecoach but did not tell about there being Union soldiers among them. Arrested and in possession of a large amount of money was the only reason everyone thought she was collecting for the Confederates. She told them that after the building where she was being housed collapsed, she was taken to the Confederate camp unconscious and held against her will. She was working at the Eldridge Hotel in Lawrence when the Confederates burned the city. She told them, "That is where my hands got burned and scarred." She showed them the scar marks on her hands. This went on day after day. She never wavered from her testimony.

Her jailers stoically said nothing. Through the nights when she was confined back in her jail cell, she longed for James and wondered why he had not been to see her. Was he trying to help her be free? Did he miss her as she missed him? Did he know she was scared? Did he even know she was still alive, or did he think of her as already dead?

She sat on the cold damp floor trembling and wondering how long it would be before they would hang her. She was still hooded. She heard the boots on stone as they came down the long hallway toward her cell. She heard the clunk of the key turning in the lock. She heard them enter the cell. A man grabbed her, pulled her up, and pushed her out the door. She stumbled as he pushed her up the stairs. He bounced her off the door, causing her great pain to her shoulder. Once out in the courtyard, she felt the heat of the sun through her hood. She had not seen the sun nor the outdoors in weeks. Then the man abruptly pulled her hood off. Her eyes burned from the bright light. She saw no gallows, but before her was a large wall. *They're going to shoot me*, she thought.

The man got up close to her face, so close she could smell his breath and feel his spit. "We will be watching you. This is not over!" He called back over his shoulder, "Open up." She only then realized she was inside a fort. Prior to this, she had not known where they had taken her. He pushed her through the doorway. She tripped over the shackle chains and fell against the hard earth. As she lay on the ground, he removed the heavy shackles. Her wrists and ankles had been rubbed raw by the restraints. He then turned and left her with no further word. The great wall door closed behind him, leaving her crumpled and alone outside the fort.

Unknown to her, with no evidence against her and the desire of the questioners to be done with this so they could be a part of the prosecution at the trial of the nine conspirators going on in Washington, they decided to release her. She was free.

Looking up from where she lay in a heap, Mandy saw dark clouds overhead with a blazing orange sun showing through. She ached all over and could hardly move, but the fear they might change their minds and drag her back in was stronger than the pain. She stiffly pulled herself to her feet and awkwardly ran the best she could. Off to one side was a grove of trees. She made for them. Once in the cover of the trees, she collapsed and sat just a minute to catch her breath. Looking back at the fort, she was glad to recognize it as Fort Dodge. Fort Dodge was five miles southeast of Dodge. The Santa Fe Trail was between the two. If she could just make it to a wagon train or to Dodge, she might be able to get help. She took a second to try and figure out which way to go. Looking at the sun, she thought the sun rises in the east, but which way is south? She could not think straight. She was disoriented. Her mind was in a panic. In the end, she decided to go downhill as it was easier to walk and also because the fort was located uphill.

Amanda walked, putting one foot in front of the other, in the rising sun until the intense heat got to her and forced her to stop. Her rubbed raw ankles and bare feet were impeding her walking gait. Sitting down, she used part of her petticoat to fashion some make-shift shoes for her sore feet since the man at the fort had taken hers. She also made herself a makeshift bonnet to keep the sun off her naked shoulders.

Far off in the distance, she could see the faint glow of what she thought were the streetlamps in the city of Dodge, promising rescue. The beckoning lights glimmered as if to tease her. But she was too thirsty, too tired, and too sunbaked to continue. She could barely move. Looking at her surroundings, none of the landmarks looked familiar. Off in the distance was a moving dust cloud. Thinking it was a herd coming up from Texas, she hobbled toward it on her unsteady feet. She was sure the cowhands would help her. She was only able to make her way downhill by leaning hard on a stick she found. At the bottom, she came upon what was once a creek bed but was now dried up and filled with dust. Although disappointed it was dry and could offer no refreshing water, it seemed a good way to travel. No other trail was in sight. She had no clue of where she was going. Turning around, she worked her way to a shady depression where she hunkered down for the night.

Meanwhile, the lawyer James hired asked him to show him the way to Fort Dodge. The young lawyer was not comfortable with traveling through the hostile land by himself. James was glad to do this. He thought he might have the chance to see Amanda, if only for a moment. He missed her sorely and hadn't stopped worrying since she had been taken. Upon arrival at the fort, the lawyer officially requested to see his client, Amanda. He was brusquely informed she was no longer being housed there. This frightened James to no end, especially when no one seemed to know where she had been sent. They would only state that she was no longer there. James asked to see the captain but was refused. It was strongly recommended the gentlemen leave the fort, at gun point. As they saddled up, the young lawyer commented, "I do not like this. It doesn't feel right. I think she is here." James had the same feeling.

James turned his horse toward the gate in preparation to leave. The soldiers returned to their duties. Then James took the opportunity and swiftly turned his horse back. He quickly rode to the open window of the captain. Spying him inside, he jumped right through the window, landing at the captain's feet. Six soldiers came running in, guns at the ready.

The captain yelled, "What is the meaning of this!"

Before he had a chance to explain, the soldiers grabbed James and dragged him out to the stockade. It took the young lawyer over two hours to calm the situation down. Perhaps because it was his first real case, he was more persistent. He finally found out the charges against Amanda were dropped. He also got James released after explaining the situation to the captain, as his lawyer.

The young lawyer stood patiently waiting outside the stockade as James was ushered out. "Hey, I won my first case! The charges were dropped."

James broke into a large grin, shook his hand, and slapped him on the back. "Thank God!" However, James's celebration was short-lived when he found out Amanda had been ruthlessly put outside the fort to fend for herself. She was given no water or provisions. A woman alone in the wasteland could not survive. "It's murder!" he yelled.

The captain explained, "I have no authority over those guys from Washington. They did not inform me of her release. I do agree that a woman alone cannot survive outside the fort. That may well have been their objective. I will detach a detail to search for her. But it is likely that if she sees them, she will run and hide from them given the situation."

James was really angry. "No, thanks. I will find her myself. You have done enough." Leaving the young lawyer, James started tracking Amanda.

The hard, hot, dry wind came with the morning dawn to prod Amanda awake. She was hungry and thirsty. Her wrists and ankles still bothered her. She tried eating some berries. She chewed and chewed, but without saliva, they stuck to the roof of her mouth. She gagged. Amanda was already dehydrated. She tried sucking on pebbles to create saliva, like the cowboys told her to do. But it was to no avail. She was so very thirsty. Her lips were dry and cracked. She remembered the men in the saloon talking about drinking urine in dire circumstances. She gave it a try but didn't have anything to catch it in, and the little she could collect made her gag and spit it out.

She wandered the next day until she ended up at the mouth of a red-hued canyon. She tried to decide where to go from here. She did not recognize the arid landscape. She realized she had chosen to take the wrong direction when she initially left the fort. She was thirsty, tired, and depleted. The unforgiving sun continued to beat down, drying out her nose and mouth until they felt like gumshoe. Exhausted and panting, she stumbled to a lone cottonwood set on a tall hill and crawled under its branches for relief and shade. She fell into an exhausted dreamless sleep immediately.

Every hour or so, the sun shifted enough to burn her legs. Sliding back into the safety of the shade, she collapsed again. When the unforgiving heat of the day relented somewhat, she knew she had to find water or die. Amanda had been without water for more than twenty-four hours. She wouldn't make it much longer. She thought she could squeeze water from a yucca plant she came across. She jabbed it with her fingernails, with no result except to injure her fingers. She couldn't get it to produce a single drop of water.

As the sun set, the air cooled fast. Where it was so hot during the day, it was now decidedly chilly. Amanda tried to start a fire by rubbing two sticks together, like the cowboys in the bar claimed she could do. With perseverance, she did manage to get her measly pile of twigs lit. Her hands were shaky, and she couldn't get enough twigs to keep it going. When the first shiver hit her, she felt truly afraid. The thought of death was not as bad as the thought she would never see James again. She wondered where he was and if he was thinking of her.

Amanda thought she wasn't strong enough to fight hypothermia. She worked hard to stay calm through the night. Lying on her back, she gazed into the starry sky. The stars brought her comfort, for she thought he was sleeping under the same great sky, looking at the same stars.

The next morning brought a southern wind that filled the air with dust. She was still alive, mostly by sheer will. Traveling in the dust-filled air was intolerable. She attacked the yucca fronds again, to no avail. She later learned that most cacti, including yucca, do not produce drinkable water. She plodded on for almost a mile but got too hot and felt dizzy. She sat down to rest and found it a struggle to get up again. Each time she sat down, it was worse. She crawled under the edge of a large rock and fell into a fitful sleep. When she awoke, she couldn't move at all. She felt like crying, but no tears would come. Her eyes just burned.

Amanda started praying for rain. Miraculously, it came. A big black threatening cloud rode in from the west. The loud clap of thunder was welcoming to her. Lightning flashed, and the wind grew more furious. Wind twirled her hair as the rain began to fall. The rain felt good and refreshing as she caught the raindrops on her tongue. It cooled her blistered face and ran sweetly down her steaming body. It was like manna from heaven. Slowly, her legs regained their strength, enough so she danced an awkward dance in deference to the burning hot sun. She was again hydrated and able to regain some of her strength, but by nightfall, she was again frozen, shivering under a tent made from her skirt and two rocks. She covered up as best she could with her tattered petticoat.

The next morning after a slight shower of rain, the wind shifted to the north. The clouds dispersed, and the air smelled sweet, but she was too weak to move far. She allowed her mind to think of James. She brought back memories. She smiled at the thought of James darkening his hair to look more authoritative. She remembered how her hands turned black from the dye when she ran her fingers through the soft, thick, curly hair. She remembered his touch as his big strong hands grabbed and caressed her with great tenderness and his lips softly touched hers. She thought of his bright eyes and his sneaky smile.

In frustration, she yelled toward the sky, "Why have you not found me? You're supposed to be such a good tracker. Where are you?"

"I am right behind you."

Amanda thought she was hearing things. She turned and saw him standing about one hundred yards behind her and approaching fast. She thought she was hallucinating. It must be a mirage. *Don't go running off into the wasteland,* she prayed. She closed her eyes and counted to ten. She opened them just a slit and thankfully saw him again, only closer. She again closed her eyes. She opened them wide just in time to see him as he reached her and grabbed hold of her. He held her like a child would hold a favored rag doll, as if he would never again let her go. She felt cherished. She felt saved. Relief and passion flowed through both of them, easing pain and filling them both with renewed hope for the future.

Given Amanda's condition, James thought it best to stay put until she could build up her strength a little. Dumping some water on a rag, he started wiping her hands with the cool, wet cloth.

"No," she cried. "Don't waste the water!"

Wetting the rag again, he told her, "It's okay. There is a spring over that way. It dries up in the summer, but it has running water now after the rains. We have plenty of water. After you rest a bit, we will camp by it tonight." He gave her his bedroll and fashioned a crude tent out of his raincoat. He then went off to shoot a prairie chicken for their dinner and made a pot of the best coffee Amanda had ever tasted. By nightfall, she was showing great improvement. The unforgiving lonesome desert turned into a romantic refuge. The stress of the past few weeks fell by the wayside. Both felt the time-lessness of the desert. This was their oasis. The calm permeated their very beings. As they enjoyed the relief of finding each other, they reveled in the peace of the natural environment of the sand dunes.

James took her to the most wonderful spring she had ever seen. In the evening, they tenderly held hands by the fireside and chuckled in their enjoyment. There they talked and shared their hopes, secrets, and wild dreams.

The fire crackled merrily in the starlight. Suddenly, as if by surprise, her eyes filled with stars, and her stomach filled with butterflies. He took her lovingly in his arms. The mild soft touch of his hand on her thigh set her to shivering. Her heart started to throb, and her breathing became labored. Her body started twisting with desire.

James stopped and sat up. "I don't want to hurt you. Your skin is burned. It must be painful."

Her skin was, indeed, painful. But Amanda craved his touch more than anything. She needed him both as a man and as a protector. She longed to feel him holding her, to feel the weight of his body on hers. "I am okay," she cooed.

He smiled. "I will be careful. If I start to hurt you, just say stop." His hands moved tentatively and skillfully over her body. It was sensual and sweet. Neither of them wanted to go to sleep that night, for no dream could possibly be better than this reality.

The ride home was dry and dusty. Thankfully, James knew where they were going. Her wanderings had taken her farther away from Dodge than where she started out. They stopped for a while by a small run-down ghost town. She felt a little eerie among the rows and rows of deserted wooden houses with their roofs gone and ruined walls standing there like the skeletons of a violent past. In spite of that, Amanda wanted to stay. She wanted to prolong their time together. But James said it was time to get back. The thought of returning to Dodge sent fear through her. How would the townspeople react to her now?

They rode into town in the early morning hours. The city was quiet, the street deserted. A lone cart rattled as the milkman made his deliveries. He looked up as they passed and nodded just a little. Coming to the Long Tree, Amanda's heart sank. Taking a deep breath, she dismounted. The sidewalk was clear of debris, but stepping into the shade of the building, she discovered piles of broken glass. The railing to the stairs was broken, and the chandelier was smashed. Looking around, she wearily smiled. "Well, the bar is still intact."

She made her way up the littered stairway and hesitated before entering her room. The door was hanging off its hinges. Inside, the room was completely disheveled. Her empty jewelry box lay broken on the floor. Her mirror as well as her bathtub were broken. Someone had taken an axe to her dresser. Goose feathers covered the room, as someone had slashed her mattress. All her dresses and hats were either gone or ripped up on the floor. Looking around, she found a pair of old shoes.

The other rooms did not fare much better. Downstairs, a check confirmed that all her stock was gone. The safe's door had been blown off, and the contents were gone. She was able to scrounge around and find her coffeepot and two cups that were unbroken. "Well, at least I have a pot. It's a start."

James ran across the street and got some coffee to brew as Amanda fashioned a table out of the rubble. She found a towel and used it to serve as a tablecloth. It flapped a little as wind came in through the broken windows. She found half a candle and put it in an empty whiskey bottle. She found one unbroken chair and made a stool out of another broken one.

James brought over his coffeepot, full, along with some corn bread. "I will get your stove set up so you can make the next pot." He poured the aromatic coffee and, looking around at the destruction, softly said, "I don't think you should stay here. It is not safe."

She resignedly sipped the coffee. "This is the only place I can stay. I have found you can't run away from your past. If I left this town and changed my name, in about a year or two, this all would come up again. No, I have to face this town and these people. Here and now."

Just then, Carla, one of her girls, came out of hiding. "Miss Mandy, I thought that was you. I always knew you didn't do what they said. I am so glad you are all right. Does this mean...you didn't escape?"

Amanda broke into a genuine smile, got up, and hugged Carla. Carla had always been caring of the other girls. "No, I didn't escape. Don't worry. They dropped the charges. I had nothing to do with those people." Mandy gently touched Carla's black-and-blue cheek. "Did they hurt you?"

Carla shrugged her shoulder. "Nothing I can't handle. Things have not been good around here. The townspeople took everything that they did not break. They dragged us girls into the street. The men...aaah...beat us all up. Mary, Sue, and Dali left town. Bell is now working at the Trail's End. I was able to save a few of your things—got them hidden behind the wall in the storage room." Carla ran to her hiding place and produced a rough cut wooden box. "They didn't think it was worth anything. I found it on the floor."

Amanda smiled. "Is it?"

Carla laughed. "You should have seen them fighting over that well-polished oak change box you had. I snuck this out while they were busy fighting."

Mandy opened up the nondescript wooden box. It was filled with several large bills and one ornate broach—the broach James gave her.

Starting Over after the Civil War

The next few days were spent gathering up anything that was salvageable. The damage was extensive. What wasn't broken too badly had to be repaired as best they could. Things that needed to be replaced would have to wait until the money started coming in. There was a wealth of cleanup to do. Many windows were boarded over until they could be replaced. With the little money she had, Mandy had to restock supplies. In addition, she only had a diminished staff of girls available. They would make do. Although not restored to its former glory, the Long Tree was soon open for business. The only problem was, she had no customers. It seemed the townspeople were frightened of being seen with her. Others were ashamed and feeling guilty about ransacking her place. There were some who even felt she should have been hung. Whatever the reason, no one darkened her door.

Although a little concerned, she was not overly worried. She knew this cow town. When the herd hit town, all politics go out the window. In fact, having a bad reputation was good for business. The Long Tree would make enough from the cowhands to be in business for the rest of the year. She just had to be patient.

Yet she had to pay a personal price, that of taking on customers herself. A few of them felt the need to take out revenge on her for the fallen president, resulting in long nights. Worst of all, the men delighted in asking for her time in front of James. Mandy wanted to say no, but a girl had to do what a girl had to do. Besides, for all his sweet talk, James had never asked for her hand. Perhaps his association with her, knowing the branding of her as a Southern spy along with the accusation of her being an assassin, would result, in the end, his time as a US marshal.

If the truth were to be told, although Mandy loved James with all her heart, she never really wanted a man to look out after her nor did she want to answer to any man. She cherished her independence. It was not in her nature to act the subservient wife.

From time to time, someone would come around intimating that she got away with the assassination and deserved to be hanged. Then for a short time, people would look down on her. But she was used to that. People always thought themselves better than her.

James, on the other hand, found it hard to deal with. People were saying she was guilty and she only got off because of him. There was little comfort in knowing that was not the case and it was not true. He needed the respect from the people of Dodge. His reputation was hurt. More importantly, his pride was injured. It would plague him the rest of his life.

Time brought change. Slowly but surely, things returned to normal. The herds came through. The saloon was restored. The Long Tree thrived, and Mandy no longer entertained.

It was not uncommon for the Long Tree to be filled with soldiers since the fort was located nearby. The soldiers had very little money and less hope for the future. Most, whether Northern or Southern, had no homes to return to after the war. They had no work, just time—endless, relentless hours reliving the glory days of fighting. Mandy thought of these men as mad dogs who had tasted blood and longed for a return to the days when they could legally plunder what they wanted from whomever they wanted. They were dogs of war, who not only liked the violence of war but craved it the same way a drunk would crave a drink.

One day, a hardened soldier, a colonel, rode into Dodge. Amanda welcomed him. "Hello, cowboy."

He threateningly slapped his saber against his side. "I am not a cowboy but a soldier defending justice and humanity," he announced in a booming voice.

Mandy was a little taken aback but quickly recovered. "My mistake, sir. Let me buy you a drink to make up for my inaccuracy."

The colonel demanded her time due to his rank. He felt she could not refuse him. He whispered, "I will put this place off-limits unless you start acting a lot friendlier."

The colonel was a balding, stocky man with cold, dark eyes. He had that stance like he felt he was important and should be obeyed. He drank her booze and boldly told her what he wanted to do with her. All the while, he was preaching like a Methodist preacher. The other men in the bar bought him drinks, saying he was a hero of the Johnson's ranch. It seemed the colonel captured Sibley's supply train and burned it, and then he slaughtered his horses and mules. Mandy had gone hungry too many times to think that anyone who burns supplies and slaughtered horses was any kind of a hero. But the men felt in doing so, the colonel saved lives because the Confederates broke off the attack, having no supplies.

This oversized jerk spent most of his evening strutting and making loud proclamations about being sent to kill Indians, big ones and small ones. He said he was going to scalp all of them. He bragged that both big and little scalps would decorate his saber.

Mandy was happy when Mr. Tomson came into the bar. He carried the box Mandy had given him a while back with the dress for his wife. Mr. Tomson looked a little shaken. He had dark circles under his eyes and was about twenty-five pounds lighter than when she last saw him. Mandy told the colonel that Mr. Tomson had bought her time earlier, as an excuse to get away from him. He was mad, but she called one of her girls over and gave him her time for free in compensation.

Mr. Tomson told her, "The dress did not fit. I'm sorry. We are leaving town. I brought you back the dress and wanted to thank you for being my friend all these years."

Mandy was surprised. "You're pulling out? You just paid off your farm."

Mr. Tomson explained, "It was paid off. But I had to take out a new loan on the farm to stay out of the war."

Mandy tried to quiet him. "Three hundred dollars is not that much. I can spot you."

Mr. Tomson shook his head. "It's $600, and I don't want your money. If I can't pay the bank, I won't be able to pay you."

Upon overhearing this, one of the locals spoke up. "He paid to get out of doing his duty to the Union. Then he sent money to the

Confederates so they could buy bullets to shoot the guy he hired to take his place."

The colonel aggressively moved toward Mr. Tomson. "So you're not only a coward but a dirty traitor as well."

Mr. Tomson tried to explain that he had no desire to kill anyone. He just wanted to grow things on his farm. He started to leave, but his path was blocked. Mandy asked Sam to go for the marshal at once. The colonel was spoiling for a fight. He instructed a private to go get his rope off his horse. Mr. Tomson threw the first punch, but in his weakened state, it did little damage. He was soon surrounded. The men formed a circle, pushing Mr. Tomson from man to man, all yelling, "Mansy pansy, scaredy-cat, yellow-bellied turncoat!" The rope that had been brought in was thrown over a ceiling beam. A chair was placed under it.

Just in time, James arrived and stuck his head over the batwing doors. "Hold it!"

The colonel yelled, "You have no business here!"

The marshal responded, "I am making it my business. We don't approve of lynching in Kansas. I am the reigning authority here in Dodge."

This got the colonel's dander up. A verbal argument ensued with the people in the bar debating who was in charge. Finally, James yelled, "It does not matter who is in charge because even the military holds a trial before they hang anyone! You are breaking the law. If you all hang Mr. Tomson, I will arrest every single one of you regardless of rank."

This made all the good old boys back down, knowing James had a reputation as a man of his word. The colonel, defeated in his attempt, stomped off in a huff.

Mr. Tomson and his wife did leave town, as he ultimately lost his farm to the bank. All those years of working the farm were for naught. Amanda heard he changed his name and opened a gun shop in Hays. Amanda later bought the farm from the bank for the money owed. Unbeknownst to other, she discretely used it to open a home for unwed mothers.

The pompous colonel and his outburst were soon forgotten as the Long Tree started getting more and more customers. The main topic of conversation was the raiding of homesteads by a group of dog soldiers, along with the debate of what to do about the Indians who seemed to be rustling cattle. James spent a lot of time up north, investigating complaints. He learned of many homesteaders who had been killed by the dog soldiers. He also grew to detest the militant Cheyenne.

Amanda spent many nights trying to banish the images of those murdered homesteader families out of the marshal's mind. There were nights when the big, tough, seasoned marshal whimpered in his sleep. His continued efforts seemed useless, as the marshal never seemed to relax. He predicted at this point it was just a matter of time until they had a full-blown Indian war. No one would be safe in northern Kansas. Due to his beliefs on the matter, he forbade Amanda from leaving Dodge.

Amanda respected James and his opinions, but the bottom line was she had a business to run. It required her to go meet with suppliers from time to time. Yuengling, one of the best beer distributors still in operation after the war between the states, and Western Brewing Company called for a meeting to resume deliveries to the West. Most saloon operators who offered a top-line product planned to attend the meeting. Amanda wanted to go because Weston Brewing had a novel idea of utilizing ice from the river during winter and layering it with straw in cellars dug deep into the ground. This would create ideal conditions for the beer so it could be safely stored for more than six weeks. The cellars would be sixty degrees, warm enough to keep the beer from freezing, and yet it could be served cold. Cold beer would be a great draw for the Long Tree.

Amanda knew if she told James she was going to Denver, Colorado, he would have a fit and forbid her to go. So she bided her time until he was busy and distracted with official marshal business. Then she unobtrusively rode out of town and caught the stage to Colorado at the way station. The stage ride was nice with a cool November breeze blowing fresh air through the stage. The stage traveled past Fort Lyon, where Amanda was surprised to see a White flag flying under the US flag. The owner of the Lady Gay, explained, "The White flag flying is because the Indians who want to surrender have been promised the protection of the fort. It is a symbol to them."

Later into the trip, Amanda was just about asleep when the stage unexpectedly jerked to a halt. The sun was barely creeping over the horizon. The stage was soon surrounded by a large number of soldiers. They were well outfitted, unlike the soldiers Amanda had previously encountered when on her trip West. The group of soldiers were being led by that vile colonel she knew from the Long Tree. The soldiers stopped the stage so the colonel could have a talk with the driver. Amanda watched out the window as several soldiers tilted their hats at her as they rode by. Once the large group of soldiers had ridden past her, the stage driver came to the door and asked them all to step out of the coach. The driver wiped the sweat from his forehead with his kerchief. "We have a situation. It appears the Indians are having an uprising. The troops are on their way to settle them down. We have been ordered out of the area. We can go around and avoid the trouble by making a large circle through Colorado Springs. The bad news is this will add three more days to our trip. It will also take us into Cheyenne territory. I don't like going there with a woman on board. We can instead go back to the fort for protection. Hopefully, the cavalry will settle the uprising and we could be on our way by tomorrow."

Three extra days on the rocking stage did not sit well with Amanda. The daunting idea of becoming a Cheyenne captive was even worse. When the men took a vote and decided to return to the fort, she did not complain, even knowing the delay would make the trip useless. She now wished she would have paid heed to James's warnings.

Darn, she thought, *I hate it when he is right.* Amanda was resignedly getting back into the stage when she heard a devilish yell, followed by the sound of gunfire and a bugle. Everyone looked to the horizon, seeing smoke rising high in the sky and turning it cloudy dark. Hearing the screams of women and the cries of children, the coach driver yelled, "Hurry, let's get out of here!"

The stage lurched forward. The driver was running the horses full out in the direction of the fort. Dust poured out behind the stage. The horses' hooves pounded a fast rhythm keeping time with the repetition of the wooden wheels over the hard ground. The coach jarred the passengers as it roughly bounced over ruts in the hard packed earth. Amanda tried to hold on but could not stop from being thrown onto the other passengers. Fort Lyon was a welcome sight when it came into view.

Fort Lyon was built just like most forts. Twelve small buildings surrounded a central courtyard. All were enclosed by a large, tall, impenetrable wall. A sturdy guarded gate kept intruders out. Amanda was given a room with a view overlooking the courtyard. Looking out the small window, she saw many Cheyenne being processed to be sent to a reservation. These Indians did not look like the fierce Indians pictured in the paintings around Dodge. They looked tired, with hollow, sad eyes. Women held children as they stood in line. They were hopeless, silent children. Amanda wondered how these people could be considered her enemy. But then again, she had heard many stories about White people dying a long, painful death at the hands of the Indians. She also knew personally of women who were once captives of the Cheyenne and how badly they were treated. At the memories, her compassion for these unfortunate people melted away. This made her feel a little guilty. She turned away from the window.

That evening, the commander honored her with a fine dinner at a well-set table. She had enjoyed a long hot welcome bath, and her room had a soft bed for the nighttime. Spending time at the fort might not be so bad, she thought as she drifted off to sleep. Amanda was used to working evenings until about one thirty in the morning. She awoke hungry, as she was used to eating in the early morning hours. She knew getting something to eat in the fort after hours was highly unlikely. To take her mind off food, she decided to take a leisurely walk in the moonlight around the courtyard. With the exception of a few men posted on night duty, the fort was deserted. Amanda saw a light glowing from the stable, and she gravitated toward it. The door was open. She stepped in, and on the floor, she saw her bags sitting. She thought that strange because bags would not be generally unloaded from the stage until arriving at their final destination. Spying the stage driver greasing the front axle of the stage coach, Amanda inquired about the bags.

The stage driver explained, "We may be stuck here a few days. I thought you might need some of the things you've got in those bags. Besides, I wanted to get some weight off the coach before I jacked it up."

Amanda thought this strange as no one had actually brought her bags to her. Also, none of the men's bags was unloaded. But she had to concede that her bags were the biggest and that men had been known to wear the same clothes for days on end. So she guessed that was it. She accepted his explanation.

The sergeant arrived at the stable and ordered Amanda back to her room, saying it was unsafe for a lovely woman like her to be out alone with all the lonesome men in the fort. Amanda did not like being bossed around, but he offered to bring her bags to her room, so she agreed.

Back in her room, she could not get back to sleep. She got a chair and was looking out her lone window at the moon while trying to decide what to say to appease Jim when he found out where she was. She jumped to her feet when she saw the stagecoach moving at top gallop leaving the fort. Before she could make it out of the room, she heard gunfire. The pompous colonel who had been at the Long Tree was whooping and hollering and waving his sword around. She watched in horror as the soldiers displayed cut-up, bloodied bodies of dead Indians. She might have understood the bodies of warriors, but these were mutilated bodies of children and even babies. They were being displayed like gruesome trophies.

Amanda lay shakily back on the bed and covered her head to drown out the horror. It only took a few minutes; then there was total silence. Dead silence. Amanda stayed unmoving in bed until the commander came to call on her. She did not ask about what she had seen from her window during the night. She could not bear to think or talk about it. She just asked when she could return to Dodge.

Back in Dodge

Amanda was taken back to Dodge from the fort in a chuck wagon. James walked up just as a soldier helped her down from the wagon. He set her bags down after her. "Amanda!" James shouted.

Amanda waved him off. "Save it." She walked stiffly and purposefully away from him and into the shelter of the Long Tree.

Back in her room, she breathed a sigh of relief. All she wanted to do was to get her shoes off, curl up under a warm blanket, and take a long nap. She knew that was not going to happen when she saw James bring in her bags. For the next hour, she was lectured about all the awful things that could have happened to her because of her foolishness. Later that night after James had his say, Amanda haltingly and with distress told him about the terrible things she had witnessed on her trip.

At her description of the horrific events and seeing her agitated expression, James sadly shook his head. "There's no stopping it now. It's all-out war. What's really bad is this is not going to be a war with rules. Please, I'm telling you, stay in town. If you absolutely have to go somewhere, go in an easterly direction. It still won't be safe, but safer. The main problem is with the hundred-day volunteers. You see, they don't know anything about Indians. They have not had enough training to fight anyone. They will shoot at anything that even resembles an Indian. With people like Sherman and Chivington leading them, it was bound to happen. I will take a ride up to Fort Dodge in the morning and see what can be done. Those hundred-day contracts have to be stopped."

James's intended trip to Fort Dodge was delayed for a few weeks due to the influx of a new herd coming up from Texas and an order to stop wagon train traffic through the Cimarron cutoff because of an

Indian uprising. When he did finally get to the fort, he was informed a congressional investigation was being opened on the matter. He was assigned the job of running down and capturing the errant colonel since the colonel had left the army in disgrace. He was now wanted to pay for his infractions and injustices. It seemed the fleeing colonel had crossed over the Dead Line—an area thirty miles south of the fort and across the Kansas railroad tracks.

When a marshal, any marshal, dared to cross the Kansas railroad tracks, he was putting his life in danger. James was fully aware of that. Over the Dead Line, the desperados put up wanted posters for lawmen instead of the other way around. It was the place where more than half the US marshals who were killed in the line of duty met their end.

When James entered into the Dead Line, he found many posters with his own name on them. At first, he laughed at them. But as the reward amount increased, it was no longer funny. He had to stealthily go about his business. He managed to find the colonel hiding out in an old deserted mining camp. The colonel did not put up a fight, declaring he was justified in killing the Indians, for it was the only way to end the rustling of cattle and the raiding of homesteaders.

James stopped him by saying, "Save it. My job is just to bring people in. I am not a judge."

But the colonel was persistent. He felt a need to tell his side of things. James had seen this behavior before. It seemed the more severe the crime, the more they wanted to talk about it and justify themselves.

The colonel said, "I only had a small group of volunteers. Not fighting men at all. It was very cold—never got above freezing. Most of the time, it was below zero. That day, it was only about twenty-two. There was about four feet of snow on the ground, making movement very slow. I was told a camp of hostile renegade Indians was camped about fifty miles south of my location. These Indians were intending to make war on the Whites. They desired to drive all the Whites from Kansas. The Indians were stockpiling weapons. With the small number of troops I had, I could not protect the settlers. A lot of settlers had been brutally murdered and scalped. The Indians attacked Fort Lyon, and Major Blunt's command was to cut ribbons. I was given orders to appropriately chastise the Indians. I thought if I struck a blow against the savages and determined Indians, maybe the settlers could live in peace. None of the conversations I had with my commanding authority or with the Indian agent informed me the Indians had the protection of the fort. Actually, they repeatedly told me the Indians at Sandy Creek were hostile."

Again, James said, "I am not the judge. I just bring people in. I have seen the homesteads after an Indian attack, and I saw the aftermath of Sandy Creek. All I've got to say is I wish I had never seen either." Privately, he thought, *How could he try to say he had no idea the Indians had the protection of the fort when Indian women and children, not warriors, were inside the fort and there was a white flag flying above the fort?*

The colonel remarked with a smirk, "God save me from civilians."

James smiled just a little. His smile was forgotten as he remembered his time when he was stationed at Fort Ridgley. All in all, he was very happy to leave the disgusting colonel at the fort in custody and return to Dodge.

Dodge City was a welcome site after being over the Dead Line and dealing with the colonel. Amanda's arms were something worth coming home to. Amanda and the good marshal were busy making up for lost time when they heard a crashing sound coming from the bar below. James ran down the steps to investigate. As he did, four men, the Grasons, grabbed him from behind, throwing him up against the stucco wall. The marshal, having been caught off guard, responded by swinging wildly. Tom Grason received a blow to the jaw and fell backward, breaking a table and crashing to the floor. Lee fell off to the side. The two other Grasons grabbed and confined James, holding him soundly against the wall. Tom hit James twice in the breadbasket, before James kicked him in the crotch, sending him crashing to the floor. Lee punched James in the face. Slumping, James seemed to have the fight taken out of him. Then Jeff and Sam Grason punched him multiple times. James fell to the floor while the four boys kicked him unmercifully.

Mandy, who had followed James down the stairs at the commotion, grabbed a long-necked bottle from the bar and hit Tom over the back of his head. He fell. His brother Jeff yelled, "You two-bit whore! You're going to regret that." He reached over, grabbed Mandy by the arm, and threw her back against the wall. Mandy saw that the marshal was no longer moving on the floor. Before she could go to him, Jeff then pulled Mandy roughly over to a table, slammed her face down onto the wooden surface, and held her fast in place with one hand. He raised her dress and yanked down her undies. Unbuckling and taking off his leather belt, he yelled, "This is going to take the fight out of you." Whipping her with the belt, he grunted, "Once you get soft like a woman should be, me and my brothers are going to teach you how a real woman should behave."

The brothers gathered round the table. "Get her. Go, Tom, go!"

Amanda was able to get a good kick into Jeff's knee, just as the marshal regained his senses. He slid around using his long legs and took out Jeff's other leg. Jeff fell, crashing to the floor, and the marshal grabbed Jeff's gun. "Hold it!" he yelled as Mandy slid off the table.

The brothers were defeated and quickly arrested. They were handcuffed and taken over to the jailhouse. When questioned by the marshal, they maintained they were hired by a man they did not know, to cause havoc in the Long Tree and keep the marshal busy. James was trying to make sense of this. He asked them about the attack on Miss Mandy.

"First of all, she attacked me. It was her fault. What was I supposed to do? Let her beat on me?"

James shoved him in and locked the cell while trying to maintain his temper. "You did more than defend yourself."

Jeff snidely replied, "Well, she is one great-looking toffer."

It was lucky for Jeff that his hands were still in handcuffs, or the marshal would have knocked him on his can.

Just then, Mr. Baker came running into the marshal's office. "They hit the bank! Come quick. I think Jack is dead."

James yelled to him, "Get Doc!" as he ran out the door. Mandy sat sorely on the Long Tree floor, momentarily forgotten by her hero.

She did not know what was going on. She heard the sound of horses leaving town. Tears burned her eyes. Where was James? Didn't James realize she was hurt? Didn't he care?

Doc came running in. "Amanda, are you okay?" he asked anxiously.

She worked hard to get up. "Yeah, I guess so."

Doc looked concerned. "Come right up to my office. I want to look you over." The walk to Doc's office was painful, but not as painful as the pain in her heart. Doc was concerned about the welts on her backside, but they were not life-threatening. "I want you to take it easy for the next few days. No working and apply this salve."

Doc, as always, was gentle, kind, and compassionate. She wished her body desired him the way it desired James. She wished he was younger. How can it be that love always had to be so unkind? Doc would love to have someone share his world. He was the greatest man in the world, yet he had no one. James, on the other hand, had every woman in Dodge after him, yet he wanted no one. Love had to be the worst thing God had ever done to the human race. She shook her head. The pain must be getting to her. Or maybe it was the powders Doc gave her. Whatever, after she got some sleep, she would ask God to forgive her thoughts. Love was not responsible for all the sadness in the world. Men were.

As she went to leave, she asked Doc about the commotion that had been going on outside.

It was then Doc told her about the bank being robbed. He said the highwaymen cleaned it out and got away. "Did you have a lot of money in it? I thought you stuffed most of your cash under your mattress."

Amanda smiled ruefully. "James convinced me it was not safe to keep all my money there. He convinced me. I deposited a lot of my money in the bank just yesterday. I saved some for running expenses, but the bulk was in the bank. I can keep the Long Tree open for a while. I hope the cowboys have some money left to buy beer."

Amanda's fears about the financial stability of the town grew as the Kingstone ranch announced they could not make payroll. The smaller ranches followed suit, then shopkeepers, then the stockyards.

The town was hit hard. Amanda worried her place would be next. No one had any funds to spare. No one was coming in to spend their money at the Long Tree. The place was almost deserted. Without any word from the marshal as to the return of the money in the foreseeable future, she reluctantly decided she had no other choice than to let two of her girls and one bartender go. She spent the nights behind the bar working alone.

James was having his own trouble. The highwaymen had gone high into the hills where the ground was mostly rock, making it difficult to track them. The men in the posse were growing tired of the chase. A pounding rain washed away any chance of tracking the outlaws. James was forced to give up and return to Dodge empty-handed.

Amanda's hope of getting any of her money back was dashed when she saw James's lone figure riding back into town. Wet, dirty, and riding low in the saddle, James had the look of a defeated man. The people ran to him, hoping to get some reassuring news. James told them the outlaws got away, but he was going to wire all the towns between Dodge and the border with their description. Hopefully, the gang would stop somewhere, and a vigilant lawman down the line would pick them up. At this news, a panic went through the town. Amanda was glad to see him return anyway. She had missed him terribly. Their reunion was short-lived as the marshal was soon called to Fort Dodge to assist in the rounding up of civilian gunrunners.

The bank finally obtained funding from Topeka and was paying off bank patrons ten cents on the dollar. If you took the deal, you could not claim any money later if the recovery of the stolen money was made. Amanda decided to wait it out rather than settle for the lesser amount.

Moving Forward

Amanda had enough money saved to buy next month's supplies, but not enough to have it shipped to Dodge. She had no money to hire the two drivers it would take to transport the needed supplies. Replenishing her supplies was crucial to business. So for a reduced price, she hired the meanest man she knew and planned to drive the wagon herself. She reasoned a trip to Ellsworth through the Cimarron cutoff would not take her that long, and she would be back with her supplies before the busy marshal found out about it and could put a stop to it. A lot of people warned her not to go. They cautioned her it was too dangerous. They said the ruffian she hired could not be trusted alone on the trail. But Amanda felt she had no choice in the matter. Without supplies, she would be out of business. As a safety precaution along with her normal concealed weapons, the Derringer and the Sharps, she wore a Colt Dragoon revolver on her hip. She brought along her big brush comb with a weapon hidden in the handle and poison tips. She wore a pin fastened to her hair that was also a dagger. Her hat was secured with a foot-long hairpin. Lastly, she took a fan with razor-sharp edges composed of daggers and solid steel ribbing. She hid a sword in her umbrella and, oh yeah, a razor in her shoe.

It would be wrong to say Amanda got up early that bright Sunday morning of the precarious trip. The fact was, she never went to bed. When the sun peeped over the horizon, she made her way down the dirty streets of Dodge, stepping over drunks asleep on the sidewalk and dodging puddles of vomit. Even though her stomach was in revolt, she knew every one of those drunks represented a nickel in her pocket. As she entered the stable, she became angry, for in front of her was a team of large oxen tethered to her wagon.

In the wagon sprawled out was the man she hired passed out and smelling strongly of cheap whiskey. Knowing how violent men could get when awakened from a drunken stupor, she chose to address the stable owner.

"Sir, can I inquire as to why I have oxen instead of the horses I bought hitched to my wagon?"

The station owner smiled. He pointed. "That man said you hired him as your guide."

"That's true. I did. So?"

"He sold your team and replaced them with those beasts of burden to pull your wagon. If your intention is to pull a heavy loaded wagon over uneven ground, the oxen will serve you much better than that team of riding horses you owned."

"I guess he did an even-up trade?" Mandy queried as she thought of the high price she paid for those fine high-stepping Kentucky Saddlers.

"No, he said you would make up the difference. That will be $10, please."

Amanda fumed. She felt like fighting with this horse thief, but because she was anxious to get on her way, she reluctantly paid the man the $10 and climbed up on the wagon. Although a little afraid as she was not familiar with driving oxen, she thought, *okay, okay, I just tell them, "Go." Then I tell them, "Whoa!" and they will go and stop right where I want. How hard can that be?* She slapped the reins, but nothing happened. She slapped them again, and again got nothing.

The stable manager laughed at her. "You have to grab them by the yoke and bow. Simply use your good stick to hit them on the legs or use the whip. Let me put on this nose basket. That way, it will be much easier to keep their attention and keep control."

The nose basket sent chills down her spine, remembering when a customer had long ago once used a nose basket on her. She could still feel the whip of a long time ago rip at her tender skin. It bothered her a lot to use one on any animal. If only she did not need her supplies so desperately.

Jumping off the wagon, she determinedly went to the front, looked those bulky beasts of burden in the eyes, and tried to explain her need for cooperation. The beast on the right raised his huge head at her, knocking her backward and sending her into a bale of hay.

That's it. She'd had it. She grabbed hold of the stick and hit the animal on the rump as she took a solid grip on the yoke with her other hand. Surprisingly, the oxen moved forward, dragging her off her feet and almost stepping on her. Getting back up onto her feet, she again grabbed the yoke with unyielding stubbornness, and off they went.

As the stable owner closed the stable doors after them, he saw Paul, the man Amanda hired, holding his sides and laughing in the back of the wagon. The stable owner thought to himself, *I think Miss Amanda Arness has met her match.*

Amanda rigorously dragged those large oxen through the narrow path up one mountain and back down another. The sunset, when it finally came, was a welcome site. Her whole body ached. She was stiff and sore. And she was still angry. She was about to climb into the back of the wagon to rest her aching, blistered feet when Paul jumped up.

"No! We are not stopping. We must make it through these flatlands before sunrise." He lifted the struggling woman onto the wagon while she was yelling to high heaven. He clamped put his calloused fingers over her mouth. "Quiet now. We do not want the Indians to hear us. Just lie down and shut up. You know, any decent woman would have given up long before now. If we live through this stupidity, that marshal of yours is going to shoot me dead for going along with your insane plan."

Amanda tried to calm down and sleep, but every time her eyes would begin to close, the wagon would hit a rock, and she would be roughly tossed high into the air, sending more stabbing pain through her already-aching body. She rolled to the left then rolled right. There wasn't any place on her body left to bruise. She tried hanging on to the wooden side of the wagon, to no avail.

They hit so many disruptive bumps she began to think he was doing it on purpose. When the sun retook the sky, Paul climbed into the wagon and said simply, "Your turn." Then he lay back and pulled his hat down over his brow.

She stumbled over the uneven ground, half the time holding on to those troublesome beasts. Realizing they seemed to know where they were going and still a little afraid of them, she mover farther away, just touching them softly when they tried to come to a stop. This seemed to work out well. As the hills turned into hot flat ground, Paul started to sing rowdy tunes at the top of his voice. She stomped to the back of the wagon. "Are you touched?" she asked with a profound sense of injustice. "You told me not to talk, yet here you are caterwauling at the top of your lungs."

Paul sat up. "We are now in Indian territory. Slaves walk while men ride. The Indians know we are here. They will think twice about taking a man's slave. If they approach us, I want it to be for the reason to buy you. If they think me a fool, all the better. Get a move on, girl, before I take a whip to you to show the Indians you are well trained. It will get me a higher price."

Amanda was about to hit the roof. "You…" she sputtered.

Paul jumped off the wagon and menacingly raised his hand to her. He growled, "You get out front and work that team. Don't dare raise your voice to me, or the Indians will think me weak. Trust me, the best bet we've got is them thinking me a little bit touched and you not worth the trouble. They do not like oxen, and the wagon is empty. So move it before they decide to take payment for trespassing."

Amanda was still hopping mad but, upon consideration, thought it best to go along with Paul. *The oxen would not be able to keep up this pace much longer. We will rest soon*, she thought. She continued to trudge along while Paul sang. The oxen seemed to respond to Paul's singing. That just made her madder, for the song he chose to sing was "Mandy, really handy when the marshal wants some candy. She makes him feel dandy when she brings him brandy. She gets a little dirty and acts a little flirty."

Paul changed the last line though. He sang, "The marshal going to hang me from the highest tree. People gonna come and see the marshal hanging from a tree because he killed me."

Amanda shook her head and began to sing, "The marshal's going to hang you on the lonesome prairie because of the way you treated me. No one will see, so the marshal's not going to hang from any old tree."

Thinking of different ways James could kill Paul made the day go easer for Mandy.

When Paul allowed her to rest the team, she commented, "I thought the trail would be more level and accessible."

Paul laughed. "Is that what the good marshal told you? Well, it is not level but rather composed of immense undulations. It has a hard, dry surface of fine gravel, incapable of growing anything. The general features of this whole great desert its sterility, dryness, and unconquerable barrenness, with no water for man nor beast. We will travel at night, for the sun of the day will burn our eyes and take the hide right off you."

Amanda went to take off her shoes when they rested. Paul stopped her. "The Indians will smell your feet. Best leave them on."

The following day, Amanda was trying to get the oxen to move through a valley of rocks while the man she hired again lay singing at the top of his voice in the back of the wagon.

From out of nowhere, a group of six Comancheros surrounded them. One man came up close to her. He put his revolting hands on her breast and rump. The man gave them a rough squeeze as the man she hired kept on singing. Her captives brazenly slapped her on the rump and remarked, "Fine woman. Will bring me a good price when I get tired of her."

The men examined her more, lifting her dress and poking at her waist. A fight ensued among the men as they debated the order in which she would be taken. One man addressed Paul, "Is it okay with you if we play with the woman?"

Paul raised his bottle to them. "Women are a dime a dozen. Have at it." Mandy sputtered.

The Comancheros laughed. "Not White women, at least not around here."

Paul stood and scratched his jaw as if he was thinking. "You know, you're right. So you all best get off her." Paul pulled two six guns and fired at point-blank accuracy. With the rapid fire, he killed all six in one thunderous second.

Looking at Amanda half dressed, he yelled, "You're not hurt. Get up and get moving. They might have friends."

It was only years of training that stopped Amanda from crying. She got to her feet and began again, tiredly putting one foot in front of the other. They were lucky to find a small spring to water the oxen. But they couldn't stay there. When the sun came up, they encountered a group of Indians. Once again, Paul acted like a drunken fool. Catching them off guard, he killed five of them. Unfazed, he returned to his singing.

The sun relentlessly burned hot and bright in the sky. They pulled the wagon between two rock outcroppings. Paul made a makeshift tent out of a tarp to shield them from the sun's rays. Every part of her body hurt as she lay on the hot ground. She finally spoke to Paul and requested no singing.

He laughed. "The Indians are afraid of people who are touched. They consider us taboo—bad luck. They will prefer to stay away from us. They will look for a better target before they come after us. The bigger fool they think I am, the better and safer it is for us. It is better to be a fool than be a dead hero."

Thinking over the day's events, she had to agree. Far too soon, the sun retired for the night, and they were off again on their quest. Finally, Bent's Fort came into view. Mandy was relieved.

The fort was one of the few White settlements on the Santa Fe Trail. It was built of adobe bricks, 180 feet long and 135 feet wide. The 15-foot walls were 4 feet thick. The men bragged that it was the strongest post west of Fort Leavenworth. Amanda thought the large prairie cannons posted on hexagonal bastions at each corner was a bit of an overkill.

When she remarked so, one of the men remarked, "The Cheyenne are teaming up with all the other tribes. They attack, and you won't think there's enough cannons."

Amanda smiled. "I stand corrected. Without a doubt, that is true. I am very tired. Is there somewhere I might be able to rest?"

The man showed her to a room inside the walls that faced inwardly on a plaza. She finally had some relief from the hot sun and a comfortable place to sleep. She was able to wash up and have a meal. She had just fallen blissfully asleep when two mountain howitzers fired off. The sound was deafening. She jumped up and ran out into the plaza.

Men were running in all directions, all armed. Paul saw her in the middle of the fracas, reached out, grabbed her around the waist, and threw her to the ground.

"What's happening?" she demanded as she hit out at Paul.

"The Comanche, Kiowa, and Cheyenne are attacking the fort. You can either help or find a hole to crawl into and hide. But running around out in the open is stupid."

Amanda conceded. She spent the rest of the day pouring hot lead into molds to make bullets. When the sun rose on the third day, it found her carrying water to exhausted men.

The Indians had at last been turned back, and the fort was still standing solid with only three killed and twenty-five wounded.

A meeting was held late that afternoon, as Amanda tried to get herself presentable. It was decided the fort could no longer be used as a trading post. The Indians, although having been fought off countless times in the past, had managed to cause so much havoc so as to stop the supplying lines. Therefore, the fort was deemed useless and was set to be destroyed.

Mandy and Paul left the fort under military escort. Thankfully, Amanda was able to ride in the wagon this time as the commander ordered some of his men to accompany them and handle the oxen. They had traveled about three miles away when the soldiers blew up the fort, rendering it useless. There was a bright light illuminating the sky as rocks and debris flew high into the air. Hot cinder-filled smoke surrounded her wagon.

The Indians, realizing the soldiers were abandoning the fort, launched an attack against the leaving military soldiers. Her lungs pumped like bellows in a foundry while the world suddenly became very quiet. The only noise she could hear was the commander yelling orders to his men. Uncertainty and trepidation took control of her mind. As the band of about a thousand Indians grew near, she became exhausted emotionally. The past few days had been too much to comprehend. Something about the thought of dying had sapped all her strength. She wanted to stop and hide. The wagon was moving faster than she thought the oxen could ever move. The soldiers dismounted and formed a circle with her wagon in the center. She lay low in the back. They fired in rotation, slowing down the Indians. It was the large cannons that saved the day.

The soldiers rode with them until they reached the fort at Pinon Canyon, where they departed ways. Paul wished they had taken them somewhere else, anywhere else. The fort was built by means of what they called "eminent domain." In other words, to build the fort, they had to confiscate the land from Indians, farmers, and ranchers who weren't willing to sell. This caused bad relations between the residents of the fort and those who had lost their land. Peace was tenuous at best. There was no feeling of safety at the fort.

The only good thing about going to the fort was that Paul was able to get some of the needed supplies from the soldiers.

While there, Paul introduced Amanda to Tom Tolian, a hardened man who was a tracker, US army scout, and occasional bounty hunter. She had heard the name before in the Long Tree. If she was to believe those wild tales of the drunken Texans, Tolian was one of only two men to ever escape alive from the siege of Turley's Mill during the Taos Revolt. Mr. Tolian was currently out of work due to the fall of Fort Bent, as he supplied the fort with whiskey and flour. As such, Amanda was able to hire him to procure and bring the needed supplies to the Long Tree.

The US government was enforcing laws prohibiting the importation of alcohol into Indian-occupied country, causing Tolian to smuggle his alcohol from the Missouri frontier and risk confiscation or obtain alcohol from Mexico which had no such prohibitions.

Alcohol trade expanded enormously during these years. With Amanda as a backer, Tolian would be able to expand his business to include other products, unfortunately most of which were taxable. Tolian solved this problem by concealing his more valuable merchandise in a secluded hiding spot somewhere along the trail before customs could examine the wagon. He seemed to have an uncanny knowledge of when the US marshal was out of the territory.

With Tolian now bringing the needed supplies to the Long Tree, Amanda wished to return to Dodge. Paul did not want to return, but he knew Amanda would not make it safely there on her own. It also occurred to him that the US marshal might not take it well if he abandoned the marshal's girlfriend.

So Paul made a deal with a horse trader for some fast-riding quarter horses instead of the oxen—billed to Amanda, of course. He told Amanda they would have to travel fast to get out of Indian territory. Amanda was not willing to leave without her wagon. An argument ensued, but Amanda's stubbornness would not waver. Paul tried to explain that the Indians would not be taken in by his fool act this time.

Amanda said, "Good. That means I can ride."

Paul was not happy but agreed. "Well, the good news is we only have to travel 225 miles to get home," Paul said.

As they thankfully left the fort, a very mild breeze came sweeping up across the prairie, causing a curtain of dust. Visibility was poor. She could feel the dust on her teeth and in her pores. Looking around the countryside, she was surprised. While this time of year usually brought migrating birds and others teeming with song, she heard but one bird.

She saw a burrowing owl making its nest in a prairie doghole. Wildlife was practically nonexistent. Normally, the air carried the gentle fragrance of spring. But here, the smell of gunpowder hung in the air. She could taste it on her lips and felt the burn of it in her eyes.

"How is it possible that so many people are willing to die for this land full of dust?" Mandy said as she tried to clean the dust and soot from her eyes.

Paul looked mournful. "Before the soldiers arrived, it used to be blanketed with native short grasses, leafy trees, and full of wildlife. I bought a background map. Its intended use was to allow soldiers to track friendly and hostile force movements. If it is correct, we might make it to Springfield by tomorrow night. We must ride hard. It is about sixty miles."

The trip took much longer than Paul expected because he went out of the way to avoid hostiles. He kept on the move most of the time, sleeping only for a few hours at a time. Running by moonlight was not advisable, yet it was needed. The trip took a heavy physical toll on them that would be talked about for years.

An Embarrassing Adventure

The night grew cold. Dodge stetted down for the night. The only one on the street this night was James, making his rounds.

Paul rolled into town on the wagon, yelling at the top of his lungs. "Where is Doc? I need Doc. It is Miss Mandy. She needs Doc."

James came running. "Paul, what's wrong? What happened to Mandy?"

The wagon pulled up in front of Doc's office. Paul was still yelling for Doc as James climbed into the back of the wagon. Doc came running down the stairs. Paul yelled, "She is awful sick, Doc!"

Doc said, "Let me in there." Climbing in the wagon, he noticed a strong smell of whiskey. "How much has she had to drink?"

Mandy spoke up, "I'm not drunk, Doc. I merely spilled it."

"Where does it hurt, honey?" Cowboys and townsfolk now surrounded the wagon, trying to get a glimpse of Mandy and find out what was going on.

Mandy said, "I hurt everywhere. Get me out of the street please."

Doc told James, "Take her up to my office."

James complied but had to hold his breath as he picked her up and carried her up the stairs. She stunk bad. Real bad. There was a strong smell of bad whiskey, vomit, poop, dried blood, animal, buffalo hides, sweat, and French perfume. After depositing her onto Doc's table, he retreated outside for some fresh air.

James saw Paul sweeping maggots out of the wagon, then stomping on them. James's stomach was still churning from the odor. He asked him, "What happened to her?"

Paul said, "I think she had better tell you that her own self." Now Paul, who was never one to keep silent about anything, wandered off down the street, shaking his head. "I ain't never going to take a shemale along anywhere again. Never in my born days have I seen the like."

James returned to Doc's office. Doc was rolling up Mandy's soiled dress. He handed it to James. "Take this out and burn it," he said as he removed a large pot of hot water from the stove.

"This is a really expensive dress and one of her favorites. Maybe it can be washed?" James said while holding his nose.

Mandy, shaking while under a sheet on the exam table, said, "Burn it. I don't ever want to see it again."

"Is she going to be all right? What is wrong?"

Doc answered, "I don't know yet. I am going to need some time alone with her. However, I do not think it is anything life-threatening."

It was about two o'clock in the morning when Doc finally came out of his office. James came rushing over.

"She is fine. I need a drink," Doc said as he rushed over to the Long Tree.

Paul followed them in.

James asked, "Will someone tell me what is going on?"

Doc answered, "I cannot say exactly. She is going to be fine. I have given her something to help her sleep."

Paul said, "That sure is good to hear. I can't tell you how scared I was."

James asked again, "What happened?"

Doc looked over at Paul. "You tell it. She is my patient."

"She might get awful mad at me talking out of school."

Doc said, "She thinks you are some kind of hero. I tried to tell her you got her into that mess in the first place. She would not stand for it, said you saved her."

James was getting down right mad and wanted answers. "What happened!" Their loud conversation drew the attention of the men in the Long Tree. Even Sam stopped pouring drinks and moved to their side of the bar.

"Well, Miss Mandy asked me to take her to Ellsworth through the Cimarron cutoff. She had to get a shipment of supplies for the Long Tree. She almost took my breath clean away when I saw her come down those stairs wearing that green dress with all those ruffles and lace, you know the one." James nodded. Paul continued, "We were having a real good time singing and joking. It got hot. Mandy turned white, but her cheeks turned bright red. She had that look a woman gets, you know, when she's ahh…"

James interjected, "It is not her time for another week."

Doc spoke up, "Sometimes when it gets real hot, it can bring it on early."

Paul continued, "Well, she had me stop a few times so she could go into the woods. She was not looking good, holding her side and being so pale. Even though it was out of our way, I took her to the way station, thinking a drink might help. When we got there, she gave me her flask and asked where the outhouse for women was. They only had one privy. It was about 150 feet from the station, but you could smell that thing from the porch. I watched her as she headed for it so no one would bother her. This thing was about 4 feet by 3 feet and made out of oak that was weathered. She was wearing that bulky dress. The door was about eighteen inches wide, and the dress would not fit through the doorway. She bunched it up in the back and squished it in through the door. Once she got in there, she could not get turned around because the dress took up the whole thing. Well, after some time, she managed to get turned around. The dress was still sticking out a bit and holding the door open. She finally closed the door on the dress. Thinking she was okay, I headed in to get us some whiskey.

"Just as I was finishing my drink, I heard her screaming. I went running out back to the outhouse. This thing was made for men with large broad backs. It seemed that, being a petite woman, her backside was smaller than the hole. She fell in. Well, only partway. My guess is the dress held her up from slipping any farther in. Anyway, she was stuck in the hole. Well, I did not know what to do. Those men from the station were standing around laughing, and Miss Mandy was getting madder and more embarrassed by the second. I cautiously opened the door, and all I could see was her petticoat and that large dress. It took me a while to find her as I was trying not to look, don't you see?" Paul looked embarrassed and said, "I did not mean anything improper. I was feeling around with my eyes closed. Next thing I know, she hit me and sent me sprawling clear out the door."

The bar erupted in laughter. James shifted his weight. His eyes grew narrow.

Doc smiled. "So that's how you got that black eye."

"Well no, Doc, that was not it at all."

Doc tilted his hat, rubbed his mustache, winked at James, and said, "I am going to regret this, but how did you get her out?"

"Well, I was coming to that if you just let me finish. Some of the other fellas and me tried to pull her out. By then, she had sunk down so far there was just no way. That's when we decided to knock the outhouse over and push her out."

James said, "You knocked the outhouse over with Mandy in it?"

"Well, yeah. It was the only thing we could do. Don't you see? We decided we had to knock it over frontward because if we knocked it over backward, she would still be stuck. Frontward, she would roll out."

Doc mused, "That makes sense. No, no. What did I just say? Sam, I need a drink if I am going to make it through this."

Sam was leaning on his elbow, staring at Paul. "Hey, everyone, get your drinks now. I am not going to miss this story."

Paul said, "Well, Sam, I could surely tell it better if I was not so dry."

Every man in the joint offered to buy Paul a drink. That is, everyone but James, who was trying to picture his Mandy sitting in an outhouse, waiting on these men to rescue her.

Sam poured Paul a drink, and everyone in the place watched as Paul downed it.

Doc said, "Come on, get on with it. I have to go check on my patient soon."

"Well, like I said, we decided to knock the outhouse over front-ward so she would roll out. We knocked it over, but she did not roll out. The thing was positioned over the hole in the back, so we men turned it and slid it around. The outhouse fell apart as we were doing that and came crashing down on her. The seat board of the outhouse cracked, pinching her backside. Well, James, I did not have any choice. I pushed her out. I had to. But I did not look. Honest, I did not see anything."

The men from the bar were now whooping and hollering at the thought of Paul's hands being on Mandy's bare behind.

"When she got free, she was madder than a wet hornet and went running off toward the wagon. Then I noticed her drawers were down around her ankles. She kicked them off. I was not sure what to do. I didn't want to leave them there, even though they were kind of soiled. I gathered them up and put them in the wagon."

Doc said, "It was the only thing you could do." James agreed. "So how did you get that black eye?"

Paul replied, "I am coming to that."

Doc asked, "You mean there is more to this story?"

"Yeah, I ain't told you the half of it."

Doc muttered, "Sam, I need another drink."

After every man in the bar had another drink, Paul continued. "So we got back on the wagon and headed out. I noticed that Miss Mandy could not sit still. She kept fidgeting. After a while, she admitted she had gotten a splinter in her backside. You know those weatherized oak splinters could be painful and dangerous. She could not reach it."

James sputtered, "Are you telling me that you…?"

Doc spoke up, "Weathered oak splinters from a privy could be very dangerous and should be removed as soon as possible."

"Like I said, she could not sit on the buckboard. Well, we decide she should lie down in the back of the wagon, on my uncured buffalo hides, until we got to a town where we could get her some help."

James was thinking. *No wonder, she smelled so bad. Buffalo hides that were uncured!*

"She was looking none too good. We came to this abandoned farmhouse. They had an outhouse. Miss Mandy said she needed to use it. I checked it and did not see anything wrong with it except some traps hanging from the roof. At least it didn't smell as bad as the one at the station, and it had a small hole. She was in there quite a while. I figured she was having trouble doing her business. Miss Mandy came running out of that thing, yelling at the top of her lungs. Seems there was a hornet's nest between those traps. It fell on her. I had to soak her down with well water to get those things off her. Then she took to shivering, had belly cramping, and lost her lunch. She had bites and stings all over her, so I took her over and rolled her in the pigpen."

James raised his eyebrows. "You rolled her in the pigpen?"

Doc asked, "Why in tar nation did you do that?"

Paul answered, "To kill the sting poison. There's nothing better for bee stings than mud. There weren't no creek around. It was the only mud I could find."

Doc concurred, "Yeah, that would draw as the mud dries. Sam, I need another drink." After a cowboy bought the next round, Doc asked, "So how did you get that black eye?"

"I am coming to that." The cowboys were having a grand old time. Each one was remembering a time when Miss Arness had gotten herself into some kind of jam.

Paul continued, "Miss Mandy is a tough old gal. She was acting like she was fine, but I could tell she had a bad fever. Thinking cold water would help, we went to the river. The river was high due to the runoff from spring. It felt bitterly cold. That mud was sticking to Miss Mandy like pine tar to a tree. She spent the better part of an hour in that frigid water. I thought it best to make camp as Miss Mandy was chilled to the bone. Her dress was covered with water crystals that danced in the light of the moon. She shed the wet dress, and I hung it in a bush to dry. Well, she was none too shabby standing there in the moonlight. Her eyes were brighter blue than the river, her skin pearly white, and that red hair. Well, let's just say she is well put together."

This brought a new round of whooping, as the cowboys imagined Miss Arness without her dress in the moonlight. James, who was not having any fun at all, stopped drinking.

Doc moved between Paul and James and inquired, "She still had her undergarments on?"

"Well, kind of. She had gone into the bushes to take care of some personal business and got stuck up in a thornbush, and she called to me for help as every time she moved, she would get stabbed by those thorns. The bush was all stuck up in her petticoat. As I pulled on the bush, the lace came loose. Then Miss Mandy ripped it off."

Doc inquired, "Her petticoat?"

Paul replied, "Well, no, the lace." This revelation brought a groan from the crowd. "I made her some supper of wild berry and river rat. She said she did not want any. I gave her some whiskey from my old stash."

James asked, "That homemade rotgut?"

"Yeah. It's not so bad when you ain't got nothing else. The night went well, except for a few bats that seemed to take a liking to Miss Mandy's hair. When the sun came up, I went to get her dress off the bush and saw a bunch of red ants all over that bush. Miss Mandy was feeling none too good. I took her to old man Dicker's place. He had a new privy build just this summer. It was all fancy with a moon cut in the door and everything. I asked him about it for her. Mr. Dickers said he had a small hole made for the misses, so he was sure Miss Mandy would not fall in. It ought to have been okay, but the door did not close. Miss Mandy gets in there, and a swarm of botflies just covered her from head to toe. We were half a mile down the road, and she still could not get rid of them. Miss Mandy said the flies were not so bad, but the mosquitoes had a feast on her. She was bitten all over."

Doc said, "I was reading the other day about mosquitoes being the cause of some sickness. Sam, I need just one more drink. Hopefully, you did not stop at any more privies."

"Well, you can't expect a lady to just squat anywhere. I was doing the best I could for her, don't you see? I found her a real good one that was used by the big shots that were building the railroad up there by Hill Junction. I checked it out. It had everything. It had a sears catalog, a moon cut out in the front, a small window to let some light in, a small hole, and a bucket of lye to put in the hole after you are done to stop the flies. Honest, James, it looked fine to me. I gather what happened is her dress dumped over the lye, getting it all over her shoes. The catalog was the home of a few mice. That was not the big problem. It seemed a snake was in there, hunting those mice.

It did not take too kindly to Miss Mandy chasing those mice off and bit her in the ahh…"

Doc said, "Upper leg."

"I didn't see the snake as Miss Mandy came running out, yelling at the top of her lungs."

James was getting upset. "Snake bite?"

"I could not take the chance of it being poison, having not seen the snake, and I knocked her down. I did not feel right about lifting her dress but figured I had to. I cut her deep so the poison would run out. Mr. Dickers said I had to suck the poison out."

This brought a new round of whooping and hollering as the cowboys thought about Paul sucking on Miss Mandy's—ahh—upper leg.

James now said, "Give me a drink, Sam."

Doc said, "It was not poison. Did she hit you? Is that how you got that black eye?"

"No, Doc, I am coming to that. Miss Mandy's leg started to turn blue where I cut her. I figured I did not get all the poison out, so I killed one of Mr. Dicker's chickens and tied it to her."

James stood up and asked, "You mean to tell me you tied a fresh killed chicken to Mandy's upper leg?"

"Well, yeah. Mr. Dickers only charged me two bits for the chicken."

The cowboys agreed that was a good price. The girls from the Long Tree could not keep up with the drink orders as the cowboys debated where on Miss Mandy the—ahh—upper part of the leg was and the use of a fresh killed chicken on snake bites. After another round of drinks, Paul continued. "Miss Mandy was looking kind of feeble. I thought she could get some help in Shaker town."

James said, "There are no women in Shaker town, just miners!"

"Yeah, I didn't think about that until we rolled into the center of town. All those yahoos were pawing at her. Miss Mandy was holding her own, kidding them and putting them off."

The cowboys gave a knowing nod. One of them stated, "Miss Arness can handle men better than any woman I know."

Paul said, "You got that right, but I thought it best to get her out of there. But those yahoos would not let us go. I pulled my gun, but someone hit me from behind. As I was going down, I saw them pull Miss Mandy from the wagon."

James was struggling to keep his temper under control. He felt an overwhelming desire to see Mandy. No one saw James slip out of the Long Tree and head toward Doc's office.

Entering the office, he asked quietly, "Are you asleep?"

"Yes," Mandy replied.

James smiled. "I was just checking on you. Doc said he gave you something to make you sleep. I know you never sleep this time of night. Are you okay?"

Mandy, sounding a little tired, responded, "Yeah. What's going on at the Long Tree? It sounds noisy for a Tuesday."

James laughed. "It is packed. They're all listening to some tall tale."

Mandy responded, "We are always low staffed on a weekday. Maybe I should go down. Sam may need help."

James told her, "Sam has them under control."

Just then, they heard a loud round of laughter coming from the Long Tree, followed by some breaking glasses.

Mandy smiled. "Maybe you should get back down there before they start shooting each other."

James took her hand softly. "I am going. Do you need anything before I go? Are you sure you're all right?"

Mandy said, "I'm fine. Get down there so you can tell me what Paul is saying."

"You know Paul. He always tells the truth embellished with a little horse hockey. You should sell a lot of beer tonight."

Mandy said, "Let me guess. His uncle went on a trip like ours. Could you send one of the girls over with some of my clothes for the morning?"

James replied, "I don't think anyone ever went on a trip like that. See you later. You can tell me the real story when you're feeling better." He made it to the door, turned, and looked at her with sad eyes. "Did those men from Shaker town hurt you?"

"No, I told them you would shoot them. They were not impressed. They said you're a lawman and would not do anything. After some debate, they decided if they hurt me, they would have to kill Paul, and then you would hang them. I also offered the bigger ones a free trip upstairs of the Long Tree when they're in town. The bell rang, and they all had to go to work. It seems they fire anyone who misses a day. They figured I was more trouble than I was worth."

James smiled. "You do get yourself into a lot of trouble. Maybe I ought to get myself a farm gal."

Mandy scoffed. "I can see it now—you sitting at home every night, knitting on the porch. Oh no, I got that wrong. She would be sitting at home alone while you would be at the local saloon hunting bad guys."

"I bet she would be a lot less trouble than you, but not as much fun."

There was a loud round of laughter from the Long Tree followed by some whooping and hollering.

James said, "See you later, Mandy."

Mandy replied, "Later, James." She rested her head on her pillow. A smile grew on her face as she thought of James on a porch swing knitting baby socks.

Back at the Long Tree, Doc again asked, "So how did you get that black eye?"

Paul told him, "If you have to know, the wagon went under a tree. Miss Mandy ducked, and it hit me, knocking me off the wagon."

The sun was coming up. A few cowboys were passed out with their heads lying on the table. Miss Mandy came in, walked up behind Paul, stopped, put her hand on her hip, and tapped her foot.

One of the cowboys said, "She is built like a brick shithouse."

This brought a new round of laughter. Paul turned a motley shade of red and made a hasty retreat out the door. Sam handed Miss Arness the book of figures showing the take this Tuesday night. It was higher than the total from all the last weekend.

Mandy raised her eyebrows. Then she said, "I need those supplies more than ever. Anyone want to take me to Ellsworth?" There was a stampede to the door.

Paul was keeping out of James's way for most of a week, knowing James was plenty mad about him taking Mandy through the Cimarron cutoff even though the military had ordered it off-limits.

James was making his rounds when he spied Paul going into the Trail's End saloon. James followed. He knocked the dust off his boots as he entered the bar. The bar smelled of beer and wet carpet. Smoke hung like a mist over a swamp. An odor of urine came from a dimly lit area. James wasted no time turning toward Paul; his hands plunged deep into his coat pockets, clenching and unclenching his fists. His bloodshot eyes glowed with rage as his insides twisted. James hoped for an excuse to get violent.

Paul felt a tap on his shoulder, and his stomach clenched with immediate recognition.

James grabbed Paul by the collar and lifted him up off the stool.

Paul yelled, "If you will kindly let me down, I can explain myself!"

James dropped him like a wet rag. "Well?"

Standing toe to toe, both men were over six feet tall. Not a sound nor a blinking eye was evident in the joint. All eyes were on James and Paul. Paul grunted and scratched the whiskers under his chin. Then Paul cocked his head to the side and cracked his knuckles, for he thought it made him look tougher.

"Maybe we should step outside." James nodded at the door and extended his arm for Paul to lead.

Sweat poured down Paul's back. "I was broke. She offered me a great deal of money to make the trip. I never thought she would actually go through with it. I tried to discourage her. I bought the biggest, meanest oxen I could find. I figured she would take one look at them and give up. When she didn't, I started insulting her in order to get her to quit. Nothing worked."

James kept a stone-cold look of concentration on his face. He glared at Paul. "So for a few dollars, you took Amanda through the pass, knowing full well the risk to a White woman?" Looking Paul in the face, he noticed the cracks in his dried lips and the veins that littered his already-broken nose. James felt compassion for his old friend, but only for a brief moment. "Out!" he growled.

Once outside with customers circled around, Paul lunged at James. James was expecting the attack, and he easily leaped to one side. Paul fell to the dusty ground with a shocked look on his face. James pulled him to his feet, tearing his new rawhide jacket.

Paul, upon hearing the material ripping, went into a fit of rage. He pounded on James. James hit Paul hard, making his ears ring. Blood dripped from his nose. Paul's legs jellied, and he crumpled to a heap on the ground. James stepped over Paul and walked away without looking back. Paul, soaked in blood with a second black eye and half his face swollen, stumbled after him. But he took a few steps and fell. He hollered after James, "I did everything I could to protect her. She would have gone anyway with or without me!"

Mandy was not pleased with James's actions but thought it best to just let it go. Life in the bar returned to normal.

The Reconstruction

The reconstruction was going on all over the South. On the surface, this was a good thing.

Mandy was drinking her morning coffee, doing her books, when a lady slowly entered the bar. She awkwardly made her way to the table. "Miss Arness?"

Mandy looked up and recognized the woman as one of the Simons girls. They were once the biggest plantation owners in the South. "Please sit. Sam, bring another cup and some of those sweet breads."

Sam smiled, recognizing the signs of starvation the same as Mandy. The woman looked embarrassed as Mandy cut off a large slice.

"Please join me. I hate to eat alone. You looking for a job?"

The woman meekly nodded as she stared at the sweet bread.

The ice that had built up inside of Amanda all those years ago when the ladies from the plantations would act like they smelled something bad upon seeing Amanda and Kitty at the store started to melt. Mandy remembered being asked to leave the store once so the decent Simons could shop in peace. "You're Louise, the youngest of the Simons clan, aren't you?"

Louise wished Mandy had not recognized her. She also remembered a time when she would not be caught dead even sitting at the same table with one of those girls.

"You need a job? Well, I don't have anything available in the bar. But I can use someone to tend to the wardrobe of the ladies who work here. You will not make as much money as a working girl in the saloon. It will entail some fancy sewing as most of the dresses are adorned with lace and beads. You can either work upstairs or from your home."

Nick, a rude and troublesome cowboy, swaggered into the saloon. He looked over at Louise sitting with Mandy. "What's this? A new girl. I think I want that one."

Amanda promptly stood up. "She is my dressmaker." Turning to Sam, she said, "Sam, we will finish our business in my room." Then turning to Louise, she said, "If you are interested in the job, come along."

Louise did not want to leave the sweet bread, so she did not move. She wanted the job, but she was also very hungry.

Amanda realized the dilemma and smiled a little. "Sam, send up some eggs, steak, and coffee. I'm pleased to have you join me, Louise, as we discuss the job."

Louise felt exposed and uncomfortable as all the cowboys in the saloon watched her climb those stairs. Her fear intensified with the sounds coming from the many doors along the long upstairs hallway. They passed through the thick red drapes to Amanda's door. Old habits die hard. Louise feared touching anything in Amanda's room for fear that whatever low-life animal living on Amanda might rub off on to her.

Perhaps it was the flowery burgundy printed wallpaper made of heavy patterned fabric or the burned orange drapery bed hangings over Mandy's green four-poster bed that bothered Louise. Amanda got a pot of coffee from her morning stove and set out two cups. The cups had intricate blue pictures of old New Orleans on the front of them. Louise thought they looked out of place on the redwood table. She found the peach drapes on the green windows almost unbearable. Amanda was showing Louise some of the dresses she would need fixed and was explaining how the dirt from the streets of Dodge run havoc with the day dresses. Louise did not hear a word Mandy was saying but just kept perusing the room and wondering about the threadbare monstrosity carpet with great sprawling green leaves and red blotches that lay on Mandy's redwood floor.

Amanda lit several candles, explaining the coal oil lamps seemed to suck all the air out of the room. Louise thought the gold paintings made with luminous paint that reflected the light from the candles to be tacky. It would take two pots of coffee and a large breakfast before the two women began to talk of the war.

Louise finally admitted their plantation was taken over by the Blacks. "Sherman had our plantation labeled as having military value to the rebels, so Poe directly supervised the dismantling of all the buildings. The crops were burned. And all horses, mules, and wagons were confiscated along with our vegetables, apples, and our stock. At that time, we still had the land. Only the land. We were living in an old springhouse that was hidden under brush, for we stopped using it years before the war. Then came the reconstruction with Sherman's special field order, number 15. They confiscated four hundred thousand acres of land along the Atlantic Coast from South Carolina to Florida, dividing it into parcels of forty acres. Don't that beat all—them Union dogs took our land, cut up the farm, and gave it to our Negros."

Amanda did not know how to react to this. When she lived in New Orleans, she hated the large overbearing plantation owners who visited the gambling house. They had her do things they would not ask their good wives to do.

She also knew the Simons treated their Negros better than most plantation owners. She thought a farm raising cotton or rice needed to be large in order to make a profit. She wondered if the Negros would be able to grow anything on the burned ground. She knew it would take years to make a forty-acre farm profitable, if it could be done at all. "I thought Johnson issued a proclamation that returned the lands to the rightful Southern owners?"

Louise responded, "Yeah, he did. My father and brothers have returned to get back the land. But General Saxton from the Charleston, South Carolina, Freedmen Bureau's office refused to carry out President Johnson's wishes and has denied all applications to have lands returned. Father wrote and said I should look for work as it may be a long time before we can go home. I am not sure I want to go home. Everything is gone."

"At least most of your family is still alive." Amanda took a long drink of coffee. She wished she had not started Louise talking. Louise looked like she might cry.

"We lost my brothers Bob and Carl, sister Judy, and Uncle Lewis. We don't have any idea what happened to John, Paul, and Leroy. We were all kicked off the land before they came home. Maybell and her kids were forced off their land as well and went west with a wagon train. We have not heard from them, as they don't know where we are."

Mandy was actually relieved when a voice outside her door told her there was trouble down in the bar. "I am sorry. I have to get back to work. Have you got anywhere to stay?"

Louise looked upset again. "We've got a place across the tracks."

Mandy knew about shanty town. She had friends from the wrong side of the tracks. She knew it was mostly homes made of whatever discarded wood could be scavenged.

"Okay, I have a storefront down on Sixth Street. It is small, but we could set you up with a sewing machine and a weaving table. I will set you up a credit line for the supplies you need. For now, I have to get downstairs. Come by about eleven tomorrow and we will get you set up. Please stay and finish your breakfast." Amanda stood and left the room, leaving Louise alone with her thoughts.

Amanda knew Louise would move her family into the sewing house and figured she would make out in time. She would take the rent out in trade.

Once Amanda left, Louise slipped some sweet rolls into her bag. Then she washed her hands and brushed off her dress so the bugs that live on those low-life women would not get on her. She looked at a picture of James on Mandy's dresser. She investigated the looking glass and thought how much better she looked than Mandy. Younger too. Louise realized the most eligible bachelor in town was James, as he had a steady job and was not bad looking.

Louise peered over the rail as she descended the staircase. Mandy was sitting on the bar, and several men were raising their glasses to her. Louise thought, *You don't need James. You've got all those other men.*

James stood looking over the batwing doors. The men became aware of James's presence and backed away from Mandy. One lifted her off the bar and set her on the floor. Louise could not hear what the marshal was saying to Mandy but could see an attraction between the two. She thought the only way she could have the marshal was if Mandy was out of the way.

While Louise stood watching, a lady with a sparkly dress and a huge feather in her hair came in. Mandy jumped up and exclaimed, "Kitty?" Mandy's face beamed, and she looked thrilled. The two women embraced, linked arms, and came up the stairs together.

They walked right past Louise as if she wasn't even there. Louise bumped into the marshal as they both tried to leave the saloon at the same time. She smiled sweetly. The marshal smiled back and tipped his hat. Louise had noticed earlier that men did not tip their hat to Miss Amanda, either in or out of the saloon.

Mandy and Kitty talked for hours on end, catching up about the gambling house and life afterward. Mandy found out, to her dismay, that Kitty had fallen on hard times. A combination of age and a rough life had taken a toll on her. But a friendly game of twenty-one told Mandy that Kitty's hands had not aged that much. Against her better judgment, Mandy gave Kitty a job as a dealer, with the provision she would engage in no creative card playing.

KKK

Amanda and Kitty were sitting in the saloon when they overheard a group of self-righteous boors talk about running the Hester family out of Dodge. The bone of contention was that the father of the family purchased a bull that one of the men wanted.

It seemed Mr. Hester paid a little more than the bull was worth, thinking the bull could be used as a sire to improve the bloodline of his small herd. Mr. Hester was also known to hold meetings of a religious nature on Sunday mornings and Wednesday evenings. Mr. Hester was a member of the "Two by Two."

Those self-righteous boors were planning to run every last mother's son of the Hester family off in retaliation. They heard the men discuss their plans for dividing up Mr. Hester's property, including the bull.

The leader of the group noticed Mandy and Kitty sitting within earshot. He came over to Mandy, wielding a big bowie knife, reached down, and used her dress to clean it. "You seem kind of interested in our conversation. What's it to you? You got a soft spot for those Two by Twos, do ya?"

Mandy looked him in the eyes. "Ain't no Two by Two ever put a dime in my pocket. I don't care what you do to them."

Kitty stood up and was soon surrounded by this group of men. She showed no fear but said, "I was just thinking. You men just fought a war where you had to kill a whole bunch of people. I would have thought you all would have got tired of doing that. I guess you men never get your fill."

The leader twisted Kitty's arm back and stuck his fingers in her cheeks. "You best keep your nose out of our business and your mouth closed, or we are going cut that pretty face of yours up so bad that no man will look upon you." He paused, then drawled menacingly, "You know, I think this could be a fine meeting place."

Later that night after the marshal was called away on what turned out to be a wild-goose chase, several men entered the saloon dressed in white sheets and pointed hoods. Sam pulled out his double-barrel shotgun in preparation for trouble. But he was too late; one of the men grabbed it then knocked Sam unconscious. Mandy was forcefully pulled out of her office. The men in white sheets surrounded her. "We are the Invisible Empire of the South. Your place has been given the honor of being our meeting house." The men began moving around in a circle.

One stepped forward and forced her down to her knees. "You will tell no one of our activities. Absolutely no one—ever."

Another man stepped forward and placed a hangman's rope around her neck as a warning. "You will give us access to a private room whenever we request it."

Still, another man stepped forward and dragged her around the saloon by the end of the rope. "You will never speak of this." He kicked her hard, and then the group left.

Mandy rushed over to check Sam. Once he awoke, she cautioned him to tell no one for their safety. "I want to talk to James alone regarding this." Once upstairs, she checked the rope burns on her neck. Out the window, she caught a glimpse of James on his horse, riding back into town. She rushed to put out her lamp, heavily creamed her neck, and put on a scarf. If he thought she had already gone to bed, he might decide to sleep at the jail. She did not want James to ask too many questions.

Mandy did not want her place being used for the Knights of the Invisible Empire of the South meeting house, but fear and concern gave her little choice in the matter. At first, it was not so bad.

They only requested the use of one of the secluded back rooms. They even paid for their drinks. She just put bottles on the table and left the back door open so she did not even have to see them. One day, they requested the main room. Mandy had to close the saloon to accommodate them, not an easy thing for a wide-open town. She put a bottle on every table and went upstairs. Her girls had been warned to stay away. She tried hard not to hear what was going on downstairs.

The marshal returned earlier than expected from a manhunt. Seeing the Long Tree closed, he used the back stairs, wondering what was going on. In the hallway, he heard the start of the meeting going on downstairs. He tried Mandy's door and found it was locked.

Using his key to unlock it, he went in.

The room was dark. Her bed was empty. The seasoned marshal pulled his gun, for he heard a sound—breathing. The sound was coming from under her bed. He moved to the bottom of the bed. With his gun at the ready, he said in a demanding voice, "Come on out of there."

Mandy squirmed out. "Jim, Jim! I am so glad you are here! Quiet! I don't want them to hear you." Mandy explained to Jim about the clan's forced use of her place. James started toward the door. She stopped him. "I do not know if I can throw them out. They pay for the hall and the booze."

James turned, one eyebrow raised, and looked at her. "Do you want them here?"

Mandy tried to explain with downcast eyes. "It's not just the threats. They are people you know. They could put me out of business. I recognize some of their voices."

James sat down next to her. "Who?" he queried.

Mandy trusted him implicitly. Without thinking, she gave him names. "Mr. Smith from the bank. Roy Arles who runs the general store. Clamp the blacksmith. Joe Martian the mayor. And I think Mr. Cash the traveling judge. Most of the city council. Maybe that new preacher. I only heard him talk a few times, but I think he is one of them."

James knew Mandy was very good at knowing people's voices. He hated to admit the men of the Klan were his friends. Mandy tried to talk the marshal out of going downstairs, but a marshal had to do what a marshal had to do. James got up and went to the door. "After what happened last night, I cannot just let this go."

Mandy looked concerned. "What's happened?"

James checked his gun. "The night riders set the Piles's house on fire. They shot and killed him, his wife, and the baby when they tried to escape the fire. The three other children were shot as well, but they lived. I took them to Hays. I did not think them safe around here."

The news angered Mandy. In one foolish moment, she reacted by telling the young marshal to run them out of town and run them all out. James left, using the back door, then circled around, and came in the front. With gun at the ready, he walked tall, head held high. He had a feeling of righteous intentions as he kicked the door to the meeting room open. The door slammed back against the wall with a resounding thud. James demanded the meeting be ended at once.

The meeting was about to end anyway, and no one wanted to butt heads with a US marshal or his famous gun. Those "brave" hooded night riders made a fast dive for the door.

If the marshal thought that would be the end of it, he was sadly mistaken. The Klan put out the word not to drink at the Long Tree. As a result, very few patrons came in. And those who did were met when they came out, forced into a back alley, then were beaten.

Rocks flew constantly at the windows until every window was shattered. Threats were painted as a warning on the front of the saloon. Mandy had a choice to fight or run. Her first inclination was to run, but stubbornness and the lack of ready cash changed her mind. She thought about selling out. Amanda looked over her stock, knowing no one was going to pay for a saloon banned by the Klan. She made the decision to stand and fight. Step 1 was to wash and paint. This took more than a week because she would paint by day, and the Klan would repaint at night. The windows were boarded up and the door put back on its hinges.

The first herd was due to come into town. Mandy put up a sign proclaiming that drovers could drink for free. Instead of the free lunch she usually put out, she charged ten cents a plate to make up the difference. This worked. The joint was packed. The Long Tree was once again open for business. With the protection of the drovers, who were always ready to get into any kind of fight, the locals slowly started coming back in.

Amanda was surprised she was making a little profit. Perhaps having Kitty at the faro table had something to do with it. But having Kitty at the poker table had a lot to do with it.

Amanda had initially worried that Kitty would try to take over and run the Long Tree.

She needed not to be worried. Kitty seemed happy doing what she did best—keeping everyone else happy while she lightened their pockets. Mandy thought she still had a lot to learn from her. Although always the big winner, Kitty was smart enough to leave the men a few dollars when they left the table. She kept the customers happy. The local men, in particular, seemed to be having a run of good luck, always leaving the table with a few drover dollars. Not a lot, just enough to brag to their friends that they beat both the Long Tree and those out-of-town drovers.

James was very proud about how Amanda overcome the influence of the Klan. Things seemed to be going well. Kitty was so busy now she was working about eighteen hours a day. Mandy encouraged her to take some time off for herself. But Kitty said she needed to make money when the sun shone. She said she would catch up on sleep when it clouded up.

Kitty's dresses were well-worn, neat, and clean but grossly out of style. Mandy wanted to thank her for all her help but had very little money to spare as new inventory was needed and the recent profits had not been that great. So as a way to show her appreciation, Mandy offered Kitty the pick of any dress in her wardrobe. It was a way to show Kitty that she cared and also improve Kitty's wardrobe. Knowing that Kitty was a slightly larger size than her, Mandy knew she could only pick a few styles. Her choices would be limited, but the dresses were very nice and fashionable.

Kitty was very tired when she had the time to visit Mandy's room to choose a dress. All the dresses were in good shape and very nice, but Kitty was of an age where modern fashion did not fit her mature form well. After trying on a few dresses, Kitty felt tired, depressed, and somewhat put upon. She thought she would try one more dress. If it did not fit properly, she would take it anyway just to end this. The dress she picked was a soft green with darker green ribbons adorning it. It had a full skirt, and the length was good. It tightly buttoned up the back, which caused her a bit of difficulty. After getting the dress on and buttoned, she could not reach to get it back off. It was getting late, and she was just too tired to stretch any farther. She lay down on the settee to wait on Amanda to come so she could help her out of the dress. She fell asleep while waiting.

The day got long, and the room got dark. Kitty was still fast asleep. It was from the window they came into Mandy's room— men cloaked in white sheets and hideous devil masks complete with horns. Before Kitty knew what had happened, a sheet was thrown over her head. Her feet and hands were tied together, and she was harshly warned not to yell or make a sound. Bundled up and taken out the window, she was loaded into the back of a waiting wagon. A man of great weight sat on her to hold her still as they drove away over the bumpy road.

They eventually came to a large cottonwood tree growing alongside the Arkansas River, where they stopped. When the covering blanket was removed from Kitty's body, it was revealed to the men that they had kidnapped the wrong person. A heated discussion on what to do about the mix-up ensued among the men. It was ultimately decided that a friend of Mandy might actually be of better use than her because Mandy was the US marshal's friend and there could be repercussions. One of the men said Kitty was not in good favor with the marshal, and besides, all the men had daylight things they needed to attend to. They could not afford the extra time to ride all the way back to Dodge in order to fetch another woman.

Kitty looked up at the huge tree looming before her. It stood about one hundred feet tall with broad limbs that seemed to stretch to the heavens. She wondered what they were going to do with her. She wondered if they intended to tie her to the six-foot trunk and callously whip her until her skin fell off her body. It was a horrifying thought.

In spite of it all, she could not help but think the tree itself looked wonderful, all covered with rich yellow golden foliage. How could such a beautiful thing be used for such diabolical purposes?

The hooded men brought a rope and looped it around her neck. They led her over to the big tree. Once there, the men could not seem to make up their minds as to which limb was the best limb to use. Kitty, in her fear, could not think straight. She wondered if the birds and insects would make a home in Mandy's pretty dress, after she was dead. The men found a suitable limb to use. Kitty's ears and nose were already bleeding from the beatings she took while hooded. The end of the rope was tossed over a limb, and the men grabbed hold of it and pulled her up off her feet. She kicked in a hope of catching some ground as she choked. Kitty was lifted up into the air only for a few seconds, but it seemed like hours. Then she was lowered back to the ground.

Her neck burned as she struggled for breath. The men cheered and danced around a huge fire they had started, just to lift her again and drop her. This happened several times over. Finally, mercifully, she passed out. The men had their fun; the night was getting long. The fire was dying out, and so the night riders left. Kitty lay in a heap below the towering tree.

When Kitty awoke, she found the rope partially and painfully imbedded around her neck. At first, she was confused, perhaps from the lack of oxygen. She kind of thought it had been a bad dream. Once her head began to clear, she was filled with fear. She staggered up and tried to run but fell on her face as her feet were still tied at the ankles. She rolled over onto a sharp rock. She rubbed the rope around her feet against the rock until the ropes worked themselves off. The rope, having been pulled off her legs, loosened where it was tied on her hands. Again using the rock, she worked her hands free also. She grasped the rope that was around her neck using a slow and firm motion and carefully pulled the rope out from her skin. It took a long time to remove the rope. Her neck was very painful and inflamed.

Her neck was red, blistered, and bleeding from the burn caused when rope ran across her skin quickly. She carefully made her way down to the river, rinsed the burned area with the cool water, and gently removed pieces of rope fibers from the burn with her fingertips. Her neck was raw and bleeding excessively. The burned skin looked purple, deep enough for her to see underlying bones. To prevent infection, she dressed the burned area with a bandage made from a piece of her slip.

Her throat was also sore. Her mouth was dry, and she had difficulty swallowing the cool water from the river. In addition, she felt light-headed.

Kitty knew she would be unable to find her way home in the state she was in. She would need protection from the hot rising sun. Moving slowly and using leaves and branches along with the rope they had used to hang her with, she made a crude shelter for herself as best she could. Looking up at the hot sun, she wondered where she was. Not being from the area and because her head was covered when she was brought there, she had no idea which way to go. *Don't panic,* she told herself, deciding to rest this day and set out in the morning. She searched for rocks that would produce sparks, knowing the night would be cold as opposed to the heat of the day. She was unable to find any. She ripped the hem out of her new dress for a fishing line, using her earrings as a lure. She found wind-fallen branches of the cottonwood loaded with buds. The older bark was quite wrinkled and of varying shades of gray. She sucked on the bark and then made an oil from the seeds to make a salve for her neck. It seemed to relieve some of the pain.

Back at the Long Tree, Mandy was a little displeased that Kitty had not shown up for her work shift. She was not worried; she just thought Kitty must have a high-paying client to whom she was attending. When Kitty did not show up by morning, Mandy was growing a little concerned. Still, she felt Kitty would show up, drunk with a high roller in tow. Mandy went to lunch with James where she expressed her concerns. James said Kitty was not used to reporting to anyone and that she would show up eventually.

After walking Mandy back to the Long Tree, the marshal started asking people about Kitty's whereabouts. It appeared no one had seen her since the day before. With no known crime being committed, no trail to follow, and Kitty being a kind of free spirit, James returned to his duties. Checking in with Mandy late that night, he was informed that Kitty had been wearing one of Mandy's dresses when she disappeared and that the upstairs window had been opened. The funny thing was, the dress Kitty took was not one Mandy thought would fit her, and she left her old dress there draped over a chair.

Mandy shrugged her shoulders. "I didn't think that dress was Kitty's style. Live and learn, I guess. Maybe she did leave town, but I would have thought she would have taken her old dresses and things with her. She could have at least said goodbye."

James knew Kitty well enough to know something was wrong. With no clues, there was little he could do.

*****

Standing by the road, Kitty looked left then right. She needed to choose a direction. She knew that Dodge was about six miles away. If she went the wrong way, it would be seventy-seven miles till she got to Saint Johns. Kitty decided to stay by the river rather than take the road. People often settled by the river, and she needed the water to keep the pain from the rope burns down. So she started off, hoping she made the right choice. Traveling by the river was difficult due to swampy areas and mudflats. The trail was filled with wildlife and bright-colored birds. Fish were always splashing and jumping, leaving ripples in the water. She saw eagles and hawks soaring in the sky above, often flying with live catches in their talons or beaks. It would have been a nice walk if not for the devastating pain that plagued her.

On the third day of her trek, she saw smoke rising from a chimney. She decided to take a chance and head toward it but still waited until all the men were out in the field before cautiously approaching. Kitty had a good reason to be worried about the man of the house. He was indeed a member of the knights. In Kitty's weakened condition, she could only make it to the front porch of the cabin.

Mrs. Campbell heard a bump. She went out to investigate and found Kitty lying there unconscious. Mrs. Campbell sent her youngest to go fetch his father, as Kitty was too heavy for her to carry into the house.

Mr. Campbell, after seeing who it was, did not want her taken into his house. But he also felt refusing to help would make him look bad and suspicious to his wife and the marshal. He was conflicted. Mr. Campbell felt it was best if Kitty lived. Then if caught, he would only be guilty of assault. No one would care about an out-of-town saloon gal getting roughed up a bit. Mr. Campbell resignedly loaded her in his buckboard. "I will take her to the doctor in Dodge."

By the time she got to the doctor's, Kitty's neck was swelling so much she could not speak. She was unable to tell him what happened, although he could tell by the marks on her neck that it was a lynching. The marshal investigated but had little to go on. Mandy sat with Kitty night after night. Kitty was unable to eat for days and could drink very little, making her recovery slow. Once she gained enough strength to write, she asked the doctor to send a telegram to the Mayflower Saloon in New Orleans, attention to Connie. It read, "Hurt, come quick."

Mandy was overjoyed when Connie hit town. She introduced her to James as a good friend. Connie wanted to see Kitty, who was now staying upstairs at the Long Tree.

When Mandy introduced Connie to James, Connie's stone-cold brown eyes bothered the marshal. He had seen that hard look before in the eyes of seasoned gunmen. He was also bothered by her dress. It was simple street dress, not the kind worn by saloon gals. Her hair was simple in its style. She wore just a touch of makeup. When James stopped by to have a nightcap with Mandy, he was surprised to see Connie sitting in the shadows in the back of the saloon. He asked Mandy about it.

Mandy explained, "Connie is a watcher. She has been doing the job so long she can't stop herself."

James looked confused. "A watcher?"

Mandy smiled. "Yeah… She is here to protect Kitty. They will be leaving for New Orleans in a few days. Don't concern yourself about her."

The next few days, James saw Kitty and Connie walking through the town. It seemed kind of weird. They were going into every business in Dodge but not buying anything. James asked Mandy about this behavior. She explained that Connie merely wanted to see a Western town. James was not convinced. When he next saw them, he stopped them in the street. "Ladies, I understand you wish to see my town. May I escort you? It is not safe for women to be alone in some parts of Dodge. I have done my best to settle this town down. Unfortunately, I have not been that successful. It is still a wide-open town."

Kitty smiled and, in a still raspy, forced voice, answered, "Thank you, marshal. I never turn down a chance to walk with a handsome man." She then took his arm. Connie followed about four steps behind them. If the marshal thought he would get any information from either of these ladies, he underestimated them.

He gave them a tour of the town. He took them through the seedy side of town, where the streets ran deep in mud and the air hung heavy with the smell of uncured hides. Lye kettles lined the street as fat was being melted and turned into soap. He took them to the railroad yards. Sitting at the side of the street was two hundred cases of baking powder, marked "Long brothers." Joe Long was busy counting them. He said, "Good day, marshal." Kitty looked at Connie and shook her head no. The marshal noted the odd behavior.

It seemed everyone in town seemed to be too rich, and everything seemed to cost a quarter. On the tracks were a dozen of cars loaded with hides and meat and a dozen of cars loaded with flower and provisions. The muddy streets were rutted with deep tracks from wagons bringing in hides and meat. The marshal explained to the women that the wagons routinely run continuously from first light until late night. The calaboose housed drunks fifteen deep.

The marshal explained, "I can't house them all in my two-cell jail. Many reckless bad men come to Dodge along with many brave good men. Most just want to earn a little money, have a high time, and return to their homes. I try to keep the north side of town respectable." The funny thing was during the day, even on the bad side of town, the ladies were treated with courtesy and respect.

They went past a white-painted church where a preacher was heard preaching hellfire and brimstone. He stopped to address the marshal, "Good day, marshal." Then he went on with his preaching.

Kitty turned around, looked directly at Connie, and nodded. The marshal noted this as well. You could not tell it by her expression, but Connie kind of liked Dodge. It was one of only a few towns where you could hear music and chimes all day long, and no one was hiding their peculiarities. Everywhere you looked on the street, you could see gambling ranging from five-cent chuck-a-luck to thousand-dollar poker. Then there were the dance houses with men lined up at the door to get in.

The marshal offered to buy them a drink when they returned to the Long Tree. Mandy was patiently waiting for them when they returned. Sitting at Mandy's table as they sipped their drinks, James remarked, "Now that you have seen the town, I guess you all will be leaving."

Connie smiled for the first time. "It seems the marshal wants us to get out of Dodge," she dryly remarked.

Mandy smiled and tried to explain, "James did not mean that." James said nothing.

Connie said, "We will be leaving on the Monday stage. It is time we get back home. Do you think you will arrest someone soon for Kitty's attack?" Although said politely, she had that hard look on her face.

James played with his hat. "No. At this point, I have no viable leads. An arrest is unlikely, unless someone gets drunk and starts to brag about it."

Mandy knew Connie was not the kind of person to just sit around. She was a woman of action. Mandy tried to plead the marshal's case, to no avail.

The Monday stage came way too soon for Mandy. She was surprised at how lonely she felt as she watched the stage carrying Kitty and Connie move out of town. James saw her dejection and asked her to lunch. Mandy mentioned how surprised she was that those two ladies actually left town as Kitty's attackers remained unpunished. James said sometimes after a person was hurt really bad, they would not want to face any more trouble. Mandy shook her head. "Not Kitty."

When the stage stopped at the first way station, Connie got off and rented herself a horse, and Kitty went on alone.

The following evening, Deputy Harford entered the Long Tree. Mandy greeted him. "Where have you two been the last couple of days? I haven't seen either one of you."

Harford smiled as he removed his hat. "I just got back from Hays City. The marshal sent me there to fetch some government papers. And you know what? I took the Santa Fe train both ways."

Mandy smiled. "You did? That must have been fun. Better and quicker than getting there by horse. But where's James?"

"He got word that Joe Johnson was camping up by Cottonwood Falls. He went up to investigate. I will have a beer, Sam."

Later that night, James quietly and tiredly slipped into Mandy's room. He sat on her settee and had a strange look on his face.

She looked up at him from her goose-feathered bed. "Are you okay?"

James took off his boots. "Yeah." He said nothing else.

Mandy got up and fetched a bottle and two glasses. "Did you get Johnson?"

"Yeah… Killed three men. I hid in the grass and just waited for them to come out of that cabin. And then I yelled, so naturally they took cover. I cut loose with my shotgun. Tore up two of the men. Then cut down Bill Johnson with my six-shooter. Joe is in jail."

"Three men?"

"Yeah, I shot them down like they were hogs." He wiped the back of his hand across brow. "It seems like every day I am killing someone." He sounded so very dejected and disillusioned.

"I…I've never heard of you shooting anybody you didn't have to."

"No, I never have. It just a lot of killing."

"You look tired. Why don't you let me rub your shoulders?"

"That's okay. It's just that I have not slept for five days."

"Come to bed. Get some sleep. You will feel better in the morning."

It was a very long night. Mandy tenderly cradled her man till he fell asleep.

In his sleep, he pleaded, "Don't make me kill you."

"Jim, wake up. You're dreaming."

But he continued mumbling, "No, I don't want to kill you! No!"

"Jim, wake up. It's me. I'm the only one here."

Jim stirred, then jerked a little as he woke. "What?"

"It's me. You were dreaming."

Jim seemed to be having trouble breathing. "Oh yeah."

Rubbing his strong shoulders, Mandy said, "I'll get you a drink."

"No, just stay with me. Just hold me. You're what I need."

Mandy held his head in her lap while rubbing the knotted muscles in his strong shoulders. Her heart went out to this man. He was, without a doubt, the very definition of a hero. Yet so, so soft, so kind, and so troubled by doing what had to be done. As she caressed him, she sang softly to him. He fell into a more peaceful sleep.

Morning light filled the room. He kicked his feet a little before waking. Groaning, he asked, "What time is it?"

"About seven. Looks to be a nice day. Are you okay?"

"Yeah. Just had some nightmares to chase away."

"Nightmares are just terrible. Stay in bed and relax. I will go down and rustle us up something good to eat. After you have a hearty breakfast in your belly, maybe you can get in a nap before you go face this day."

James curled up in her soft bed but kept his eyes wide open.

Before she went down, she sat a bottle on the bed. "Here. A good stiff drink will do ya good."

James pulled the cork out with his teeth and took a long satisfying drink. He coughed a few times. It was potent stuff. He pushed the cork back in the bottle, setting it beside the bed. "Don't take too long."

Worried about James, Mandy rushed down the stairs. She did not want to leave James alone to long.

Sam was busy at the bar, setting up the saloon. "Morning, Miss Arness. Do you know where the marshal is? A man was in here last night, mouthing off about how he is going to trash Dodge for what he did to the Johnsons. He was talking real loud about how he was going to hunt down and kill the marshal."

"Oh! Do you know his name?"

"I think it was Jack Hillard. You know him?"

"Yeah. He is real trouble. I will tell Jim about this after breakfast."

James was up and dressed when she returned to the room. She sighed. "I was going to feed you in bed."

"It's late. I should do my rounds. Did you bring coffee?"

"Of course. Don't do rounds today. Instead, let me take care of you for a while. At least take the time to eat something. You know the town gets along just fine when you are off chasing who knows who."

"That's because Harford usually does rounds when I am out of town."

She looked him seriously in his blue eyes. "Sam told me that Jack Hillard is in town. He was telling everyone that he is going to tree the town and kill you."

James ate breakfast, chewing thoughtfully. Then he had a few cups of coffee. He stood up, leaned over, and kissed her softly. "Thank you. I don't know what I would do without you." With those words, he was gone.

Mandy stood silently, gazing out her open window as he walked out onto the sidewalk. From her vantage point, she could not see him, but she could hear the tread of his boots on the wooden sidewalk. She closed her eyes and prayed to God that he would protect him.

As she was praying, she heard Hillard yell for the marshal to meet him in the street. From her window, she saw her man, her life, walk into the center of the street. She noticed the sun was in James's eyes. His gun was not tied down. She heard James plead Hillard, "Don't make me kill you."

"Oh, I think I can take you," Hillard said as he pulled back his coat to reveal his weapon.

She could not bear to watch. She moved away from the window.

"Make your play!" James yelled. He sounded resigned and very sad.

She ran to her bed, threw herself down, and covered her head. It was no use. The blanket did mot muffle the thundering sound of two forty-fives going off at the same time. The blanket did not block out the sound of people yelling for the doctor.

She wanted to go to the window, wanted to see her man still alive in the street. Her legs would not take her. She sat waiting. If Hillard was killed, no one would come, but she would hear the men in the bar talking about the gunfight. If James was killed, Doc would come and tell her. If James was shot and not killed, it would be Sam who would come. No one came.

She did not have to be at work until dark. She crawled under the covers and tightly clutched the pillow. She wondered what job James could get if he would quit his job. A safe job—one without stress.

Mandy woke to the sound of her door opening.

Connie rushed in through the door and pushed it shut behind her. Leaning against it, she said, "Hide me."

Without stopping to think, Mandy gestured and quickly said, "Under the bed."

Connie crouched down and slid under the bed. "Don't tell anyone you've seen me."

After an hour when no one came to the door, Connie slipped out. She offered no explanation. Mandy asked for none.

"James will be coming. He sleeps here. Room number 4 is empty. How long will you need it for?"

Connie peeked out the door. "About a week. No one must know I am here." Connie ran and slid back under the bed. "He's coming."

Mandy went to the door and met James in the walkway. "Evening, Jim. I was just on my way downstairs."

James look a little unsure. "Dressed like that?"

It was then Mandy remembered she had never gotten dressed and was still in her bedclothes. "I need coffee. Are you okay? I heard the gunfight. I was worried."

James lowered his head. "I killed him. I had no choice. Amanda, that new preacher hung himself today."

Mandy looked back at her bedroom door. "Preachers don't hang themselves. It's a sin."

James nodded. "I think it was murder, but I would be hard-pressed to prove it. Mandy, both of your friends left on the stage yesterday, didn't they?"

"Yes, James. Both were on that stage. I saw them off myself. Why do you ask?"

"Oh, no reason. It was just a wild thought I had for a moment."

Just then, Harford came running into the Long Tree and up the stairs to where Mandy and James were standing in the hall. "Marshal, marshal! Come quickly. Mr. Smith from the bank has hung himself."

The marshal looked up in surprise. "What! Mr. Smith?"

"Yeah. Mr. Smith. He hung himself right in the window of the bank."

James looked over at Mandy. "I am going to wire New Orleans to make sure your friends arrived there safely." He then followed Harford out the door.

Mandy rushed back into her room. Connie was hiding behind the door. "Are you nuts? Did you?"

Connie took a bottle from the rack. "Yeah," she admitted as she opened the bottle and took a healthy swig.

"But, Connie, in my town, James is very smart. He will figure it out. He will hang you!"

Connie did not seem overly concerned. "Now, Mandy, you know we could not let them get away with what they did to Kitty. If they had not left a mark on her, we might have let it go. But every man who looks at her must know he cannot get away with marking up my girls. It is the only way I can stay in control. It is unfortunate that it happened in your town. But so be it. You know the law does not protect our kind, that we must protect ourselves."

Mandy was tempted to kick Connie out over this trouble. She thought of Mr. Jones and the fact that Connie killed him in retribution. In her mind, it was self-defense. Amanda knew there was no self-defense for a working girl. It would be the workhouse for her if the law ever found out. Still, how could she let Connie stay with her while going around killing off the most influential people in Dodge—even if they were terrible people who deserved it?

Connie must have sensed Amanda's unease. She said, "I will be leaving tomorrow night after it is dark. Can I stay here till then?"

Mandy thought about that for a minute. "It is not safe here. James is on to you. Even now, he is sending a telegram to New

Orleans to find out if you were on that stage. It is his job. I love him, and I don't want him hurt in all of this."

"His actions were expected and have been taken care of. He will get word back that we arrived safely in New Orleans. I just have to stay out of sight for another day. You have to keep the marshal out of this room."

Mandy took the bottle from Connie and took a large gulp of whiskey. "No one keeps James from going anywhere he wants to go. I will try, but I can't promise anything. You can hide in the closet or under the bed if anyone comes to the room. Try not to make any noise. I will bring you up something to eat."

Mandy made her way downstairs. She was a bit agitated but mostly concerned and unsure about the situation. She knew that if anyone found out, her relationship with James would be over.

Connie concluded her business on Saturday night. She was planning to leave town early Monday morning. She pleaded with Mandy to hide her for one more night, just so she could get some sleep. Mandy agreed, only because James would be out of town. She was relieved to see the end in sight. Then things could get back to normal.

Mandy was downstairs serving drinks to an overflowing group of customers, when shots rang out from upstairs.

"Oh no. No!" she yelled as she dropped what she was doing and ran up the stairs. She found James lying in a large pool of bright-red blood on the floor. In a panic, Mandy ran over him, yelling, "Get Doc! Someone get Doc right now!"

Cradling his head in her lap, James weakly looked up at her. "I heard something. Someone was under your bed. He shot me before I saw him."

Harford came rushing in. "Out the window," James instructed to the deputy.

Crossing over to the open window, Harford looked out and saw a few cowboys running toward the Long Tree and a lone woman slowly walking down the sidewalk in the opposite direction. "I don't see him, marshal. Can you describe him?"

Doc arrived and began patching James up. The wound was painful and bled a lot, but it at least was not life-threatening.

"No, it was too dark. I could not see who he was. All I could tell was that he was of a thin build. He was out of here so fast," James replied.

Mandy was so distressed. It was all she could do to hold back and not to blurt out that it was Connie who shot him.

James was slowly getting his strength back. He said, "My guess is he wanted to attack or rob Miss Amanda. That had to be what he was doing under her bed." James pulled himself up, headed in the direction of Doc's office. He spoke to his deputy, "I want you to take care of Mandy. If he tried once, he might try it again."

"Yes, sir. I will watch her like a hawk. Don't you worry about it."

Mandy wanted to protest that she did not need protection from the deputy but thought it best just to keep her mouth shut.

As scary as it was, James's injury was not that bad. Mandy was aware that Connie did not miss when she aimed her gun. Connie always told her never leave anyone half dead.

No witness should be left alive. Mandy knew that Connie allowed him to live for her. While sitting in Doc's office watching Doc repair the damage that Connie's bullet had caused, Mandy brooded with a deep-rooted guilt. Her heart ached not only for what happened to Jim but for the future and what could have been. She realized she had no choice. As long as they stayed together, she would have to lie to him. James had a knack for knowing when someone was lying to him. Fooling him would not be easy.

How could she ever explain to him? How could any man understand the fear a woman suffers inside when she sells herself to a man? How it's part of what she had to endure to survive in her profession? How could he understand the responsibility of a watcher?

Without he knowing, without the inner feelings, he would look at the killings as an act of vengeance. But Connie was not seeking revenge. She was seeking the protection of all the women who found themselves at the mercy of a master.

Mandy realized that the incident involving Kitty's attack had nothing to do with her profession. It did not matter. The men left permanent marks on her that would hurt Kitty's ability to charge a heavy price. It affected her entire future.

James often used his job as an excuse to break dates with Amanda and to keep their relationship secret. Their relationship could hurt his respect and career. It was the same thing. But she doubted he would look at it that way.

Mandy knew that inevitably someday James would ask her about Connie. She wondered if a telegraph confirming that the women arrived in New Orleans would satisfy James.

She doubted it. Unfortunately, she knew he would check with the stagecoach driver when the stage came back through Dodge. That only gave Mandy about two weeks to figure out what to do.

Later, sitting beside James as he recovered in Doc's office, James asked her to explain what a watcher was. She tried to explain so he would understand. "Her job is to watch. If there is any trouble afoot, she is to step in and stop it."

James sat up so she could look directly into his questioning eyes. "You said Connie was here to protect Kitty. Does that include punishing those who injure or harm her?"

Mandy was not sure what to say. A yes would reinforce James's suspicions. "A watcher's job is kind of like a bouncer. Connie took care of all problems that arose in the gambling house. She took care of us girls."

James saw something troubling in Mandy's eyes. "She took care of you?"

Mandy's eyes grew bigger and sadder as visions of Mr. Jones flashed through her mind. Her hand felt hot and dirty as she remembered the warm blood running over it from the letter opener. Her ears rang with the remembered sound of a thud of the barrel as they rolled it off the wagon and the splash as it hit the water. "Connie has been a watcher for a long time. She and Kitty built the gambling house together. Kitty lost it to that stupid war. Connie was able to get work in a different house. After a while, she opened a house of her own and hired Kitty. You become responsible forever for what you've built. A house provides a degree of safety not found on the streets. No one but no one marks up the girls. That is not to say it does not go on. Some men find fun in hurting a woman. If that is his pleasure, he could negotiate to do it for a price with the understanding he must not mark her in a way that would prevent her from getting future work. The law does not protect women who work in Kitty's profession. If Connie is to run a house, she must protect the girls. That is her job, and she is good at her job. If a girl does not feel safe, she will run."

James was not sure he understood what Mandy was saying. She could not be saying Connie committed these crimes and that she approved of her actions. "How much do you owe Connie?"

Mandy's stomach turned. She did not want to answer. She wanted to roll up in a ball and hide. "I owe her my life. She protected me once a long time ago."

James did not want to know the answer, but as the marshal, he needed answers. "Protected you how?"

Mandy had a flashback to the newspaper article that said the man who put those red-hot coins on her, leaving those round marks in her chest, was dead. "The law in New Orleans does not protect my kind. We have to protect ourselves."

James slumped. He grew tired and very sad. "I am the law in Dodge, and I protect everyone equally."

Mandy started to feel her anger rise because even with all of James's efforts, women were not, as a general rule, protected. If James arrested a man for beating a woman, which was very rare, the courts would let him go. If she was a working girl, the man would not even go to trial. He would just be kept in jail overnight until he sobered up. The woman, however, would carry the marks the rest of her life.

"Once a long time ago in self-defense, I killed a big shot in New Orleans. I found no pleasure in it. I had to do it. If I had gone to the law, I would have spent the rest of my life in the workhouse, if I was not hanged. Connie stepped in and cleaned it up. Another time, a man hurt me...ahh..." She could not go on. "I have to get back to work, and you need your rest." Distressed, she jumped up and quickly left.

James struggled to get out of bed. He went to the window and watched as she crossed the street and entered the telegraph office. A great sadness swept over him. He felt tired and very alone.

193

Mandy resignedly entered the telegraph office. "Good morning, Mr. Bowlen. I would like to send a telegram to the Mayflower Saloon in New Orleans, in care of Kitty Mayflower. The telegram read, "Weeds in the garden, may need to transplant."

After seeing Mandy leave the telegraph office, James, against doctor's orders, made his way over to the telegraph office. "Mr. Bowlen, can you tell me about the wire Miss Arness just sent?"

Mr. Bowlen looked at the telegraph. "Well, it does not look too confidential, so I probably could." He glanced down at it and said, "It seems Miss Arness has weeds."

James looked confused. "Weeds?"

"Yes. I didn't even know she had a flower garden. But that is what the cable said: 'Weeds in the garden, may need to transplant.'"

James thanked him and started to leave.

Mr. Bowlen stopped him. "A response to Miss Arness just came in. That was fast. We don't normally get a response that fast. Flowers must be really important to a woman."

James had learned to read Morse code while in the army. He made use of that skill now. He translated the response to read, "Transplant unnecessary. Weeds cannot grow in New Orleans. We have heavy dews and watered heavy. Believe the flowers will be okay."

Mr. Bowlen asked if James could deliver the message to Miss Amanda. It would save a trip to the Long Tree as he was expecting an important response to a cable and could not leave the office at this time.

"Yeah, I'll give it to her."

The street seemed to be five miles long as James tried to come to terms with the thought that Mandy was covering up for a murderess. He stopped on the wooden sidewalk and looked over the batwing doors. She was carrying a large tray filled with drinks through tables filled with cowboys. He entered.

Looking up, she stood still, frozen in time somewhere between her past and the end of her future. The cowboys yelled for their drinks. She jerked as reality hit her. She set the heavily laden tray on an empty table and folded her hands in front of her. The cowboys started to complain as they had not received their drinks. Mandy told them to help themselves. They started to gripe. Then they saw the look in the marshal's face and shut their traps.

The bar became very quiet as James stepped down off the stoop. He looked a lot taller than his six-foot-six frame. His face looked as if he was in agony. Blood seeping from his recent injury ran down his shirt and dripped onto the floor. He stood in silence. He did not want to confront her to hear what she had to say. Yet his job demanded that he did so. Mandy slowly turned and walked slowly up to the long tall stairs. James felt his boots had lead in them as he climbed the stairs after her.

She offered him a drink. He refused as he closed the door to her room. He pulled the paper from the inside of his vest and sat the telegram on her table. "Connie killed them all, didn't she?"

Mandy looked at the cable. She said nothing as she dejectedly sat unmoving on her bed. He stood in silence. His eyes burned into her soul. The clock ticked so loud it hurt her ears. She wanted to run. She wished her mother would come and make everything better. Guilt flowed over her like water cascading down a waterfall. The room seemed to get smaller as the walls moved in, trapping her.

"Well," he said as he tapped his booted foot.

"You don't really think I am going to answer that!"

"You knew all the time?"

"We... I could not let them get away with it. It was supposed to be me. Kitty took the beating meant for me. Kitty has always been taking beatings meant for me."

"Your loyalty to them is stronger than your loyalty to me?"

She sat in silence for a long time. Softly, sadly, she looked at the floor, not wanting to see his eyes. "Yes, when all the cards are on the table, yeah. You claim to love me yet are ashamed to date me publicly. You want to sleep with me but do not want the town to know I am your woman."

"It is more important than all that."

"In Connie's mind, she is only doing what she had to do, just like the Indians fight to protect their way of life. Like the cowboys fought the sodbusters with barbed wire. Just like the South fought the North. Those men who hurt Kitty, the night riders, were fighting the end of the South. They lost the war, but you cannot legislate beliefs. They believe by torturing me, they would save the idea of White men being superior to everyone else."

James sat down. "I don't think that's what they were doing."

"Okay, Connie needs to provide protection for her girls, in order to protect her way of life."

"You're not justifying her actions as an act of war?"

Amanda knew he would not understand. He could never understand feelings of dread, terror, panic, and thoughts of dying that a working girl felt on a nightly basis. Knowing that man she took to her room could do anything he wanted to her and no one would punish him for it. James was never forced to bow down to anyone.

He stood up and started to leave.

"What happens now?" she asked with a sense of dread.

"Unless you're willing to testify, which I don't think you are, I have no proof. I will send my suspicions to the authorities in New Orleans. Unlikely they will do anything."

After he was gone, she went to the window with a heavy heart and watched him stride across the street. It hurt terribly, like a stab to her heart because she knew her love had just ended. She sat down, closed her eyes, and began to think about their relationship. In truth, they both had been lying and hurting each other all along. She had been involved with a man who was committed to something else. He was in love with an idea. The truth was, he never truly belonged to her.

She wished the affair was not ending but knew that would not be right, good, or healthy in the long run. She would grieve her loss and try hard not to focus on the pain of breaking up. Instead, she would focus on the emotional and spiritual freedom that the end of this affair would bring her. She would no longer have to apologize for her life. She would be free to rebuild her self-respect and create a fresh new life for herself. Yes, it was time to break free. And yet how could she? Was it even possible for her life to go on without James?

She knew that ending this affair and healing wouldn't happen overnight. She would grieve the breakup because she still loved him. She would regret letting him go. She would wish they were together and cry herself to sleep. She would eventually heal and move on. She would be proud of herself that she had the courage and dignity to end the affair, and she would find someone else who treated her with respect and love.

Going to talk to James now would do neither of them any good. She spent the next week planning, drinking, and packing. During the day, she would sit and cry, sometimes unable to dig herself out of bed. She would spend hours looking out the window in hopes of getting a glimpse of James. He seemed to be staying in the jailhouse, only coming out to do rounds, then returning to the jail.

She tried to figure out how to spend the rest of her life without her love who was her best friend. They had been through so much together. She was sure he wanted to end the affair with her. It was time to let go. Mandy felt devastated with guilt and shame and was heartbroken. She felt like she had a huge gaping hole torn in her heart.

*****

James looked up from his desk at the jail. He arose and slowly walked over to get some coffee off the stove. As he poured the hot drink into a mug, he looked out the barred window and across the street at her room. The light was on. Through the sheer panel, he could see her enticing shadow moving around the room. He knew he had to end it with her.

He smiled when she came to the window and looked down at him. He thought they would have to talk. But what was there to say? She always looked a little out of place, all grown up with freckles. He thought of all the nights they spent together. She always had a thousand things to do, getting involved with drunks and wayward cowboys in the bar. All he would have to do was cross the street. They would talk about the part of her he never understood.

It was so good with her around. She always found a smile for him when days were very sad and his world was full of evil. He never ever met a person more sincere. She always listened attentively to everyone with an open mind. She was wise beyond her years. All he would have to do was cross the street and he would be close to her. And it would be so good. He would take good care of her and never let her cry, for they were so much in love.

It started to rain. He guessed it was true that you couldn't regret where you were even if life would take you someplace where you wouldn't want to be. In a strange kind of way, he was trying to let go of this woman without being angry with her. He kind of understood.

The street was turning to mud. The rain was now so heavy he could hardly make out her form in the window. Then she closed the window. All he had to do was cross the street.

A Friday night fight brought the marshal over to the Long Tree. James deftly dispersed the altercation. After the fight was broken up and the men taken to the jail by Harford, James turned to Amanda, who stood silently and ramrod straight by the back wall. He approached her and offered to buy her a drink.

Amanda tried hard to think of something to say. She drank in the sight of him. Her mind was filled with conflicting thoughts. All she could manage to come up with was "Grab a seat, cowboy. How is life treating you?" She gracefully gestured toward an empty table.

James also seemed to be out of anything to say. As he moved toward the secluded table, he responded, "Nothing much happening down on Front Street except a little rain."

They both sat. It seemed like now they were just two strangers avoiding each other's eyes. James was still believing they could make it work. Mandy was still lying to herself that she thought they could too.

It occurred to James that everyone in Dodge was killing time. No one was going anywhere. Life was just too easy here. If Mandy left, he would not miss her because the town was full of familiar faces. But even now, he told himself she would not go.

Amanda felt that by staying, she would hurt James irreparably, for he would be covering up for a murderess. She also knew he would never be out of her thoughts. He was a permanent fixture there. Bittersweet memories snuck into her mind. They let her know her life would never be as happy as it was in Dodge, for she would always love him.

Outside, autumn leaves were falling off the trees. The wind was cold, and it was raining, just a little. No tears came to her eyes as they sat with each other, drinking coffee that November morning.

There was no great big ending. No sunset in the sky to ride off into. And just as he began to say that they should make another try, she reached out across the table, looked at him, and said goodbye. The funny thing was, the world did not stop turning around. The whiskey drummer was making his delivery to the Long Tree. The cowboys were coming for breakfast. The street sweeper was finishing the street. The lightkeeper was making his way down the street, putting out the lights. Yet their world would never be the same. Sitting at a quiet table with some rolls and butter, she said goodbye. Goodbye said so easily her voice did not even quiver. Goodbye said so quietly.

The stage rolled down the street as the driver called, "Anyone for the stage going east, better get in. We're going to be leaving in five minutes."

Their eyes broke contact. He got up and held her chair. She slowly walked out the door toward the stagecoach. She was loading her bags. There was no kiss. He just held the door for her, then moved to the sidewalk. The door was closed and the step removed. The stage driver slapped the reins. The stage jolted forward as it moved down the street. Looking out the stage window, Amanda saw Louise go over and take James's arm.

She closed her eyes as the stage rolled into the sunset, and she rolled back into her past.

The End

We respectfully request you spend a few minutes to leave a review on Amazon as this will help our rating.

About the Author

Virginia Bollinger, a member of Western Writers of America, presents a unique perspective in this riveting Western, caused by the way she sees the world and a desire to share it. You can find Virginia's fan fiction and other works online under the name Gig 889.

Cindy Regis graduated with honor from Slippery Rock University and Penn State University. She has authored short stories and was previously an editor for Caldwell Education Services.

CPSIA information can be obtained
at www.ICGtesting.com
Printed in the USA
FSHW011847220421
80611FS